8/10/15

R

D1522048

Ice Games

ICE GAMES
by Jill Myles Writing as Jessica Clare

Copyright © 2013 by Jill Myles

www.jillmyles.com

Ice Games

JESSICA CLARE

MYLES | SIMS | CLARE

Chapter One

Ice Dancing with the Stars? You're fucking kidding me, right?
—Ty Randall, MMA Fighter, a.k.a. "Ty the MMA Biter," to his
manager

I REALLY HATED FAMILY REUNIONS. YOU KNOW, THOSE SHINDIGS WHERE a variety of people that would otherwise barely like each other get together and pretend to be affectionate all because of a common bond? And you're forced to sit there and endure for hours while someone goes on and on about the weather while you know they're just dying to ask you about that horribly embarrassing incident in your past but that they just haven't worked up to it yet?

Yeah. The figure skating community is kind of like that—a big family that can barely hold itself together, yet all forced to interact because of a commonality. And walking into the 7:00 AM meeting at JNO Studios and seeing a lineup of familiar skating faces? Yep. Family reunion time. And as if on cue, my stomach gave an unhappy twist. If this was a family, I was definitely the black sheep.

"Right this way, Miss Pritchard," the assistant at my elbow said, and led me to the far end of the long table where the other skaters were already seated. I was the last one there. Bad luck. My juju was already off to a bad start. I took a sip of the iced latte clutched in my hand and tried to play it casual, though internally I was sizing up the others. I thumped into my seat—last one on the right, also bad luck, but I wasn't in a position to complain, and I certainly wasn't going to demand a new seat.

My days of demanding things? Pretty much over. Now I was lucky to get scraps.

The others were dressed in business suits or designer clothing. No one had given me *that* memo. I'd thought from the phone call yesterday that this would just be a quick overview session, nothing more. Lovely. I was wearing a hooded sweatshirt, a tank top, and leggings, because, well, that was what I always wore. My dark hair was pulled into my normal tight bun and I wasn't wearing makeup. Everyone else looked like they were heading to a Hollywood party.

Discomfort made my skin prickle, but I pretended to not care in the slightest, giving my latte a long, noisy slurp in response as continued to size up everyone in the room. Five other skaters, and they were all giving me wide, too-fake smiles.

"Zara, it is so good to see you getting back on your feet," exclaimed Emma Rawley, seated at the far end of the table. "Did you just come straight from the ice?"

Mentally, I ran down her list of accomplishments. Two-time Olympian, one-time bronze medalist. She'd come in first at Nationals only once. She was good, technically, but uninspired. I slurped my drink. "No."

Next to her sat Tatiana Bezrukov, a Russian champion with a bigger pedigree than anyone else. She simply watched me, saying nothing. Tatiana was never much of a talker. She kind of let her accomplishments speak for themselves. I was surprised they got as big of a name as her, though. She was a big deal in her home country.

The three men were Serge Volodin, Toby Bell, and Jon Jon Miller. I didn't know them nearly as well as the women, but they were all very familiar to me. Very familiar and very skilled. But none of them were nearly as notorious as me.

Goody.

Jon Jon sat next to me. He leaned closer, skipping all pretense. "So… just so you know. The executives really frown on it if you walk off of the ice while on the show. I hear you're bad at that."

I shot him the bird.

"Now that's a familiar gesture." Jon Jon winked. "Nice to see Zara Pritchard hasn't changed that much."

Dickhead.

The others chuckled, except for Emma, who frowned unhappily at the table and then turned to me, beaming a smile that seemed sincere. "It is really great that you're here, Zara. We heard you'd been teaching out in Ohio?" Her brows went up, encouraging me to answer.

"Tutoring," I said, hoping they'd leave it at that.

"Anyone we know?" asked Toby.

"Nope."

He gave me an impossible-to-read look. "So an up-and-comer?"

You could say that. Most of the kids I tutored at the mall ice rink were four- to six-year-olds. I was sure they'd be up and coming at something at some point. So I merely sipped my drink and tried to look mysterious. Let them wonder.

No one had to know that Zara Pritchard had fallen so far. No one but me. This was my chance to redeem myself, anyhow.

Before they could question me more, four men and a woman, all dressed in business suits, entered the meeting room. Immediately, all of the skaters stood and straightened, and I could practically see them putting on their performance faces. Whoever had just walked in was important, which meant I needed to impress them. I slid my cup under the table and stood as well, wishing that I hadn't brought it with me. I didn't care about impressing the other skaters, but management? Management was important. They were the ones that had brought me here, and they were the ones that could boot me back to obscurity again.

A meet and greet commenced, and the suits welcomed the skaters, shaking hands and chatting. It was clear everyone in the room knew each other except for me. Not a surprise. This was the second season of *Ice Dancing with the Stars*, and the first one had been a mild hit for the network, so we were round two.

One of the executives came over to me, extending his hand to shake. "Zara Pritchard. I remember you. It's good to see you here."

My latte was sweating all over my hand, so I transferred it to my other, wiped my wet palm on my sweatshirt, and then extended it to him, hoping that didn't look too awkward. "Thank you, sir. I'm very excited for this opportunity. I won't let you down. You won't be sorry."

He took my hand and shook it with a nod. "Of course."

"I've been working extra hard since I got the call," I told him quickly. "Practicing my triple axels and toe loops to make sure I can keep up with the show. I'm used to putting in at least fifteen hours a day, so whatever you need, I can do. You can just point me to it, and I'll be good to go. I'm really versatile, too. Any sort of routine you need—"

He was starting to get a glazed look in his eyes, and I knew I was babbling. But the truth was, I needed this job badly. And I couldn't seem to make myself shut up, despite the pitying look that Jon Jon was giving me over his shoulder.

"I have lots of ideas for choreography, too," I gushed, helpless to stop my nervous babbling. "That was one of my specialties when I was competing. I tend to score very well artistically. Not that my technical scores weren't great, of course. I mean, they were. It's just that I really prided myself on my artistry, and so—"

"Who's this?" The female executive cut me off, moving to the man's side. She gave me a cool look up and down.

The man gratefully snatched his hand back and put it on my shoulder instead. "This is Zara Pritchard. She's filling in for Svetlana, since she's too pregnant to compete."

Yes! Thank you, Svetlana, for getting knocked up. I totally needed to send that woman flowers. I gave the female executive my best beaming smile.

"She's awfully young," the woman said, frowning as she considered me.

"Oh, I just look young," I explained hastily, and gestured at my tight bun. "It's the hair. It makes my face rounder than it really is. Everyone always talks about how I look like I'm fourteen, but I'm really twenty-five. I get carded all the time. I—"

The female executive sniffed. "They told me you were an Olympian."

"I am. Was." Oh god, the horrified look on Jon Jon's face had turned to one of pity. Please, please don't let me babble out my past. "I competed in 2002. Salt Lake. I was thirteen and—"

Her eyes widened. "You walked off after you fell. I remember."

Oh god. I was going to barf. "It was a mistake," I blurted out. "I was a kid, and I was really upset. I didn't realize what a mistake it would be. I'd never do it again if given the chance to do-over. I mean, no one does that, right?" I gave a high-pitched, nervous laugh. "That's like, rule number one of figure skating. You never walk off the ice mid-routine, but I did it. So yeah, I…um, won't do it again."

Please, floor, swallow me up now.

She gave me a tight look. "See that you don't."

"Of course not. Absolutely. You can count on me. I—"

She turned away before I could finish. Ouch. "Let's start the meeting, shall we?"

Everyone returned to their seats, and none of the other skaters would look in my direction. My cheeks burned with humiliation, but I forced myself to sit. I would never run away again, after all. I'd learned my lesson.

I was thirteen when I'd won at Nationals, and fourteen for the Salt Lake Olympics of 2002. I was a favorite for the US, and I had been all over Sports Illustrated and figure skating magazines, and my managers were in talks with multiple sports companies about endorsement deals once I medaled at the Olympics. I was a prodigy. I was young, cute, and everyone loved me. It wasn't a matter of 'if' I medaled, but when. I was the favorite going in.

And I'd been cocky as hell, too. I was so sure that I was going to mop the floor with the others that, after I'd skated a flawless short program, I was positive that I was unstoppable. I might have even skipped a practice.

But the ice had been shitty, and I'd drawn the bad luck of going first. Skating first, when the ice wasn't all torn up and malleable, *sucked*. I didn't like that. Bad luck all around. And then I'd doubled a triple toe loop. And got pissed at myself. Why was I doing such stupid moves? Why? Why wasn't I paying attention?

And then I'd gone into my double-axel sit spin, a move I normally nailed…except I'd mis-timed it and landed flat on my too-proud ass in front of the judges.

And then I'd sat there, humiliated, as the music played on. Skaters are taught to get up and carry on, salvage the program as best they could. Keep your chin up and your head held high, and you'll at least finish with grace.

But I'd been fourteen, and my dreams of medaling had just come crashing down around my ass. And so I picked myself up off the ice and flounced right off of the rink.

People had been stunned. No one walked off the ice. No one. They started to boo.

I then shot everyone the bird, full of myself and humiliation.

Of course, that had just made things worse.

The Olympic favorite had just scratched.

It made headlines everywhere. ZARA PRITCHARD WASHES OUT, complete with pictures of me storming away, my middle fingers in the air. My coaches were horrified. My parents were, too. The rest of my team, devastated. I'd embarrassed everyone. Worst of all? I'd killed my career. My management team fired me. Endorsement deals that were practically inked had dried up overnight. No one would hire Zara Pritchard, supreme loser. No one wanted anything to do with me. After a few years of struggling, I'd landed odd jobs skating as mascots (always masked and covered head to toe) or doing private lessons. I barely scraped by.

So now, here I was, more than ten years later, being given a second chance because Svetlana had gotten too pregnant to compete. And I was determined not to screw this up this time, damn it.

Zara Pritchard had learned her lesson.

"So," the female executive said, taking a seat at the head of the table and flipping through a packet of notes. "We're all familiar with the layout of the show, right?"

I wasn't. I didn't watch last year's show because my hated nemesis, Penelope Marks, the skater who'd taken the gold the year I should have had it, was also one of the judges. Hated Penelope. HA. TED. But I guessed that I should have paid more attention to the show. Now wasn't the time to ask.

"There will be six weeks of shows, since we're a summer replacement for the network." The executive continued on calmly. "That means six routines with your partner, provided you last the entire six weeks. You'll have two weeks, starting tomorrow, to train and warm up with your partner. Then, we start live shows. As a reminder, if you get to the finale, you automatically get a fifty-thousand-dollar bonus. The winner gets a hundred thousand, as does the celebrity. Of course, they'll be giving theirs to charity." She gave us all a wintry smile. "You are encouraged to do the same, if you choose."

Give away a hundred grand? Hell no. That'd set me for years. I pressed my lips together tightly, just to make sure the protest didn't blurt out of my mouth.

"Costumes will be provided. Simply inform production of your choice at the beginning of the week, and they will take care of the rest. Ditto with music, so we can ensure that we get the appropriate rights to play the music. You don't want to sub out at the last minute." She gave a pointed look at Serge.

Ooo, someone got busted.

"You'll be assigned the same choreographers as last year."

Assigned choreographers? I felt my enthusiasm dim a little. I loved doing choreography and expressing myself artistically through routines. Having someone else pick out that stuff for us took a little of the joy out of it. But beggars couldn't be choosers, and I was certainly the beggar here. I said nothing.

"The celebrities for this year have been selected. I realize not all of you will be pleased with your choice of partners, but we've made every attempt to be fair to all involved. We trust that even if you don't appreciate your choice in partner, that you will maintain professionalism and make the best of things. Your role as the skater is to make the celebrity look good. That means that the choreographer will be choosing routines designed at a much lower level of expertise than you are used to. We expect you to pace yourself accordingly.

"Schedules will be provided by the production assistant assigned to you. As a reminder, since we are working on a truncated timeframe, all parties have agreed to stay in the assigned production dormitory. There was an issue last season with alcohol and a few missed practices." Again, she cast a scathing eye down the line. "So I trust that will not be an issue this year. As a reminder, camera crews will be filming any and all interactions. You will essentially have no privacy for the next eight weeks. Again, I trust this will not be an issue."

She flipped more papers. "You'll meet with your celebrity later this afternoon. From there, you can get started. Any questions?"

I raised my hand.

All eyes turned to me. "Yes?" The woman's voice was cool.

"You say this is ice dancing, but I'm a figure skater. Does this mean we'll have no throws or jumps at all? Those are against the rules in ice dancing."

Emma's eyes widened, and she gave me an imperceptible shake of her head.

Uh oh. I began to babble again. "I mean, not that we can't do that. I'm totally fine with that. I was just curious, because the rules of ice dancing are different than regular pairs skating, and the skates are different. Ice dancers use a different toe pick, and—"

"It's just a name," the woman executive said in a voice that so wintry that I expected ice cubes to fall from her mouth. "You'll do regular figure skating. The name is simply for the show. Now. Do you have any *other* questions?"

I had a million, but even I knew when to keep my trap shut.

The executive smiled. "Good. Welcome to season two of *Ice Dancing with the Stars.*"

Chapter Two

I can't believe my management team stuck me with this ice dancing bullshit. I might as well turn in my man-card now. Ice dancing. Seriously? I plan on getting drunk the entire time and staying that way. —Ty Randall, Pre-Show Interview

THE 'DORM' WAS AN INTERESTING SET-UP. IT WASN'T AN ACTUAL dorm, but a series of houses about an hour outside of LA. A driver took us to the residences, and we were assigned numbers. I had 'cabin' number six, which turned out to be a small ranch-style house larger than my parent's home back in Kentucky, and it was fully furnished. The style was an interesting sort of trendy deco, complete with checkered tile on the floor, kitschy rugs, and weird lamps hanging from the ceilings. Hey, at least it was free.

I explored the house, my suitcase parked near the door. The kitchen was state-of-the-art and stocked full of health foods. Fresh vegetables, organic whole grains, oatmeal, fruit, the works. Good. I'd filled out a questionnaire with the production assistant assigned to me prior to being flown out for the show, and they'd wanted to know the kinds of foods I liked to eat. They'd listened well, too.

There were two fridges, though. I pulled open the door of the second one and peeked inside to get an idea of what my partner was like.

It was full of beer. Jesus. Corona, Red Stripe, Guinness, Rolling Rock—you name it, it was in there. I scowled at the sight. Was I being stuck with a drunk? It was important to me that we looked good when we competed. I wanted to be asked back for next season, damn it. The fridge was also full of prepared foods, and I pulled out the first box. Pizza rolls? Hot dogs?

This would not do. I immediately pulled out my cellphone and called the production assistant assigned to me.

"Hi Zara," Melody said eagerly. "What can I get for you?"

"The other fridge. It's full of garbage."

I could hear Melody flipping through her notes on the other end of the line. "Garbage? I'm not sure—"

"Beer, Melody. It's full of beer and pizza rolls. How am I supposed to ice skate with someone if they're full of beer and pizza rolls?"

"Well, you each filled out a questionnaire," Melody said uncertainly. "Your celebrity requested those things—"

"Come and get it all out," I told her. "I'll have a nice chat with my partner when he gets here. But I want it gone."

"I can't do that, Zara," Melody said. "I'm sorry. My orders were to stock the fridge with the requested items."

I frowned, and then an idea struck me. "No worries. I'll figure something out." I hung up before she could ask what, and spent the next five minutes wiggling the fridge out from the wall. When there was enough room to reach behind, I grabbed the plug and yanked it out.

We'd see how my celebrity friend liked warm beer and spoiled pizza rolls. He'd have no choice but to eat health food if that was all that was available.

Satisfied with that solution, I grabbed my suitcase and headed to the rooms. Neither one was labeled, but one was clearly much smaller than the other. That one had to be mine. I looked longingly at the larger room. It had a wall full of windows that overlooked a woodsy, grassy backyard. Pretty. My room had no windows, since I was just the lowly figure skater. Whatever. I spent the next several minutes unpacking. My skates were the last to come out, and I caressed them lovingly before putting them in a place of honor on a hook on the wall. Skates didn't touch the floor outside of the rink. That was bad juju, and I was mindful of my juju.

Speaking of rinks. I left my room and headed to the back of the house.

There was a sliding glass door off of the kitchen, and a concrete path leading through the grasses off into what looked like an enormous shed twice the size of the house in the distance. I opened the door and stepped out, and then looked down the row of cabins. Each other cabin had an identical shed. That must be our private rink. Smart. We didn't have to share the ice with the other celebrities. I was glad, though I was surprised at how much money they'd put into the set-up of things. This had to cost a pretty penny. Ratings must have been better than I thought. With a skip in my step, I headed down the path and peeked in the door.

The rink was small, but usable. A long row of mirrors lined the wall, and a barre was attached. There was a locker room on the far end of the building and off to one side, there was an electronic stereo set-up for the music. Nothing fancy, totally serviceable. I still liked it, though. My own private rink for the next two months. Heaven.

I just had to put up with some beer-swilling pig of a partner and all of this paradise was mine.

MY PHONE RANG AT 3:00 PM CALIFORNIA TIME, AND I YAWNED, ROUSING from my nap. I wasn't used to the hours here, and was still exhausted despite it being early afternoon. "Hello?"

"This is Melody, calling you to remind you that the celebrities will be arriving in a half hour. Please be ready to meet your new partner. There will be camera crews at hand to film your reaction."

"Got it. Thank you."

I got up and put a bit of makeup on, and I smoothed my bun again, making sure I looked presentable without being too eager. I hated that I had been dressed so casually this morning. If I dolled up like crazy now, the other skaters would smirk endlessly at my obviousness, and I didn't want to be on their radar any more than I already was. Still, I added some lipstick, since there would be cameras. Okay, and a bit of mascara. I had big, dark eyes, and it wouldn't take much to make them pop.

I went outside and walked down the street where the others were converging. There was apparently a clubhouse at the end of our private little neighborhood, and I guessed we needed to head that way. Stuffing my hands into the pockets of my hoodie, I sauntered toward it.

Cameras and people were everywhere, and I saw one cameraman split off and immediately head for me. "Zara," the cameraman said, waving me over. "Let's do an interview."

Interview? Bleh. Part of the job, though. I put on my best smile and shrugged. "I'm game."

"Okay, great. Why don't you tell us what it feels like to be part of the *Ice Dancing with the Stars* team? Please include the question in your answer and speak in complete sentences if possible to make it easier for the production crew."

Oh. Okay. "Being on the show is an amazing opportunity," I told him, and I wasn't lying. It seriously was.

He gestured his hand for me to continue talking.

Oh. Someone wanted me to actually keep going? Normally everyone couldn't wait for me to shut up. "Well, actually, I'm super nervous," I said, and gave a little bounce as if to illustrate this. "I've never been on TV and it's been a while since I skated in any sort of professional capacity, so this is a big deal for me."

"But you were in the Olympics back in the day, right?" he interrupted, still filming me.

"Oh, yeah." And I grimaced. "We probably shouldn't bring that up, though."

"So have you ever skated doubles?"

"I have not skated doubles," I told him. "This is actually a little different, because it's ice dancing. Doubles is two people on ice, doing a coordinated routine together. Dancing is, well, dancing." I didn't bring up the fact that we weren't even really doing ice dancing, just a mutated version of skating doubles. "You're constantly in touch with your partner, which means you both have to be in time with the music, except there are two pairs of skates to keep track of instead of just one. It requires a lot more paying attention, because you're only as strong as your partner."

"Let's talk about partners. Are you excited to meet yours?"

"Excited? I'm not sure if excited is the word I'd use. Nervous, yes. But not sure if excited is the right word. I'm mostly ready to get this thing started." I bounced around again, unable to contain my anticipation. "I know everyone says they're here to enjoy themselves, but don't get me wrong, I'm here to win this thing. I'm ultra-competitive, and I tend to hyper-focus on things. So I plan on working from sun up to sun down to make sure that we totally rock this thing and get all the way to the end. I'm not going to settle for second best. Not from myself, and not from my partner."

"Great, thanks, Zara."

"Of course. Any time you need an interview, you just let me know. I aim to please." And I'd kiss all the right asses if it meant being here next season.

He left my side and went to go stand with a few of the other cameramen, so I wandered back to the other skaters. Emma beamed a smile at me. "You ready to meet your celebrity?"

Man, everyone was sure focused on the whole celebrity thing. "I guess? I just hope he can skate."

Emma didn't look worried. "They can. That's one of the criteria for being on the show. They have to pass a physical and a rudimentary skating test. That, and they have to be someone people would be vaguely interested in seeing compete." She gave me a fainter grin. "But their idea of skating prowess and ours is a little different, so just be sure to have low expectations."

"Low expectations. Got it."

"I am really glad that you're here, Zara," she said in a soft voice. "I wasn't kidding. I always thought you got a bad rap. I mean, how many of us have wanted to walk off the ice after a bad performance?"

"Yeah, but I was the dumbass that did it." I shrugged. "And I learned why you don't, but I learned the hard way."

"Well, I don't think you should be punished for the rest of your life just because of something you did ten years ago," she said softly. "Oh well, anyhow. I'm glad you're here. Svettie was wanting that baby for forever, so I'm really glad she's getting it, and I'm glad you're getting your second chance. Just hope you don't get stuck with a loser for a partner."

Emma sure was being friendly. It was good to have someone on my side. "How do they pick the partners?"

She made a face at that, her eyes still scanning the horizon—likely for the incoming celebrities. "Oh, that. They pretend like it's all random, but it's really not. They select who you're going to be paired with based on who they want to succeed."

My eyebrows drew together. "You mean it's rigged?"

She laughed. "It's TV. Of course it's rigged. They're looking for optimal entertainment value, you know. Like you? They picked you because even though they want a good skater, they also like drama. You have the potential for drama. That's also why they like Serge." She nodded down the line at the men, who stood in a cluster, talking together. "Ten bucks says they're going to give him someone sexy because he slept with his partner last year. Made a lot of tabloids. My guess is that they want him to sleep with his partner again."

"And you? What kind of partner did you have last year?"

"I got paired up with a guy that played a dad on TV. Older. Very sweet. If I get paired up with an older guy again, I'm guessing that's my demographic. Feel-good." Emma shrugged, but she didn't seem upset by that.

"And Tatiana?"

"Tati is…" she trailed off, then looked over at me. "Well, looks like we'll see very soon. I see the limos pulling up. Come on."

The group moved into action. Cameramen surged forward, and I followed Emma as a line of black sedans pulled in. They stopped, and the first driver got out, tricked out to the nines in a black suit and hat. He adjusted white gloves on his hands for maximum effect, and then went to open the back car door.

A woman got out. Tall, beautiful, slender. She was dressed in a white pantsuit that left her entire back bare, oversized designer sunglasses, and too-bright red lipstick. It was immediately obvious who it was—Annamarie Evans, who'd been on the cover of every fashion magazine for the last five years or so, until she'd been usurped by a bustier, younger model. It happened a lot in her business, and my guess was that she was here to try and get herself a bit of attention.

The cameras loved her, though. She smiled and nodded and gave a swing of her lovely hair, stepping gracefully toward a chalk-marked X that had been drawn on the asphalt for her to go stand on when she'd exited the car.

I was guessing I'd just spotted Serge's partner. She was gorgeous.

The next limo contained another familiar figure—Michael Michaels. His black hair was cut into a mohawk, and spikes stuck out from both of his ears. Tattoos covered his neck, and he wore a black t-shirt that had the arm holes cut all the way down to his waistband, which was also covered in spikes. He wore a pair of tight leather jeans and big, buckle-laden boots. He also looked incredibly skinny and pale. I had his CD in my car at home.

Next was a woman I didn't recognize. She had blonde, wavy hair and wore a dark polo shirt and jeans. She wasn't exactly dressed like Annamarie the model. I wondered what she did.

Emma obviously knew. She leaned over to me. "Julia Mckillip. She's a racecar driver. One of the few female ones."

O-kay. That was an interesting choice. "And she ice skates? Huh."

The next car held an older man with a plaid shirt, a cowboy hat, and a beard. I could almost hear Emma's sigh of disappointment. "Louie Earl. Country singer. I bet he's mine."

I bet he was, too.

The next car held a younger girl, no more than sixteen or so. I recognized her, too. Victoria Kiss, a teen star with a few kid's movies under her belt and an equal number of accompanying kid's CDs. Not surprising, either. I wasn't really seeing A-listers. I was seeing washed up, washing up, or looking to move up on the rather tough ladder in Hollywood.

I considered Michael Michaels. If Louie Earl was Emma's partner, either the rocker was mine or the next guy. I didn't have anything against Michael Michaels (other than his dumb name), so he wouldn't be so bad.

"Last one," Emma murmured, and I turned back to the end car, watching as the door opened.

I didn't have to fake my gasp of surprise. Neither did anyone else. We were all genuinely shocked at the man that came out of the sedan.

Ty Randall, a.k.a. "Ty the MMA Biter."

Oh, Jesus. That was an…interesting choice.

Michael Michaels had been lean and skinny. This guy was neither. Tall, but he seemed more muscles than anything else. His shoulders were broad, but he wasn't bulky, and he moved like, well, a warrior. He had a big, thick neck, big thick legs, and a shaved head that held a five o'clock shadow. His face was impassive, not clearly defined, and one of his brows had a scar through it. His nose had clearly been broken more than once.

Ty Fucking Randall.

I didn't watch Mixed Martial Arts, but I sure knew who he was. Everyone did. He'd made headlines about a month or two ago when he'd been headlining a fight in Vegas, and he'd bitten his opponent. Bitten. As in, chomp chomp. As in, tore a hunk out of his nose. People had been scandalized, and he'd been put on hiatus. No one wanted to fight him. It wasn't exactly that you were expected to fight clean in MMA, but you didn't tear your opponent's face apart. I mean, Jesus. He'd made public apologies through his reps, but the incident was still too new and fresh on everyone's minds for this to be anything besides a shock.

And I was filled with a cold ripple of dread, thinking of all the beer in the fridge. Something told me that Michael Michaels wasn't going to be my partner. Oh no. Oh, nonono.

I didn't want to be with Ty the Biter.

It was clear he didn't want to be here. He leaned against the sedan and crossed his legs, and then crossed his arms over his brawny chest. He looked bored. Pissed.

He wouldn't want to win. I had a feeling he was just here for some good PR. He sorely needed it. But my guess was that he'd also be just fine with last place. Not me. I needed to win.

If he were my partner, I was screwed. Goodbye, second chance at a career. Hello, skate monitor at the mall once more. Or skating as Hildy the Pink Dinosaur in the local production of *Dino Friends on Ice*. Again.

A woman with a big poof of feathered blonde hair came out from the other side of the cameras. "All right. It's time for the team assignments! Are you ready?"

It seemed to be a rhetorical question since no one was answering. I waited, tense as hell, for the assignments.

"Tatiana will be paired with Michael Michaels."

The two moved forward and joined hands. Tatiana did a cute little twirl and beamed at the cameras. Michael Michaels just looked kind of bored. Okay then.

"Victoria Kiss will be paired with Toby."

She grinned and moved forward, putting both of her hands into Toby's, and then leaned forward to kiss him, her foot popping up. Cute.

"Julia McKillip will be paired with Jon Jon."

Julia wasn't a showy type. She moved forward and shook his hand, and then they stood next to each other awkwardly.

"Annamarie Evans will be paired with Serge."

Annamarie didn't walk—she glided forward, and Serge pulled her into his arms and dipped her. Hams, every last one of them.

The only two left unclaimed were Louie Earl and Ty Randall. I looked at the two, and then had a new appreciation for Louie Earl's stouter figure and his bushy beard. I could work with that. I knew I could. Being on a heartwarming team wouldn't be so bad, and if the public loved us, we could do well even if we didn't win. I could still be called back.

"Ty Randall will be paired with Zara Pritchard."

And just like that, all my hopes and dreams shattered. Shit. Shit shit shit.

He strolled forward to me, all cocky walk. I moved forward and offered him my hand, wishing I could summon up some enthusiasm for our pairing.

I had none to offer.

Chapter Three

So I met my partner today. She's the mouthiest chick I've ever met in my life. Won't shut up for five minutes. Seriously. Stick up her ass, too. Determined to win this thing. Like it's a real contest or something? Come on. We're going to prance around the ice in skates like a bunch of goofballs. —Ty Randall, Private Conversation with his Manager

"HI, I'M ZARA," I TOLD HIM, TRYING TO IGNORE THE CAMERA TWO inches from my face. "Nice to meet you."

He grabbed my hand and shook it, lips twisting into a slight smirk. "Ty."

"I know who you are. So, you excited to be on the show?"

"Am I excited to be on the show?" he mimicked, mocking my high pitched, slightly-nervous tone. "Do I look like I'm fucking excited?"

I dropped his hand like I'd been scalded. "Then why are you here?"

"I'm here because I have to be. No more, no less." He glanced around, his gaze lingering on the slinky Annamarie. "Parts of it might be interesting." He glanced over at me and seemed less enthused. "I'm not wearing fucking sequins or feathers, though, so get that shit right out of your head."

"Oh darn, I guess this means I'm not going to have a lot of opportunity to use my Bedazzler," I said sarcastically. "Gee, and here I was so looking forward to that."

"Ha ha." He didn't sound amused. If anything, he sounded more irritated. "Look, missy—"

"Zara—"

"Zara," he echoed. "I'm just trying to lay down the law so you know what to expect out of the next few weeks. I'm here because it's required of me. It's not because I want to dress up in a goddamn tutu and flounce around on the ice. You understand me? So don't expect too much."

My jaw set, and I wanted to kick him in the nuts for his lousy attitude. "All right then. Well, let me tell you what I'm thinking, since we're laying the law down and all. I want to win. I'm determined to win, even if I have to work *around* having you as a partner. Shit happens, but I'm good enough that I can make even a clown like you look light-footed. But let's get one thing straight. I intend to win, so don't you get in my way, understand?"

He stared at me. After a long moment, he added, "You going to fucking yap at me for the next two months?"

"Probably. And if you don't make an effort? I'm going to make your life miserable. Understand?"

Ty looked amused. "That's cute. You do realize you're ninety pounds soaking wet?"

I was a hundred and two pounds, and what did it matter? "What does my size have to do with anything?"

"If you think you're going to intimidate me, honey, it's not working."

"Don't you 'honey' me," I said, outraged.

A camera zoomed in next to my face, and I froze. I hadn't even met my partner for five minutes and we were already fighting. Well, crap. This didn't bode well for job longevity. The scathing putdown I'd been about to lay on him died in my throat. Instead, I gave him a tight smile. "We practice at 6:00 AM. Be there."

I turned on my heel and began to walk away.

"I'll consider it," he called after my back.

"Six in the morning!" I yelled back.

"I CAN'T BELIEVE IT," MY FRIEND NAOMI GASPED IN MY EAR. "YOU'RE paired up with Ty the Biter? Have you seen the internet articles on him?"

I rolled over on my bed, staring up at the ceiling, my cellphone hot against my ear. We'd been on the phone for an hour, and even complaining to my best friend hadn't made me feel better about things. "I haven't. Just that he's a fighter and he bit some dude on the nose. Give me the skinny."

"Okay." She paused for a moment, then said, "So, apparently he dates a lot of C and D list starlets. His name's attached to a bunch of famous chicks. That's why he's such a big deal."

Like I cared about that. "And?"

"And he has a type. Big. Blonde. Surgically enhanced."

"Got it. Boulders. This doesn't help me much, though, Naomi. I don't want to date the troll. I want to know what to expect when we're skating."

"I'm looking, I'm looking," she muttered. "Oooh. Let's see. He played college hockey."

I brightened. "That's a good sign—"

"Got kicked out for missing too many practices."

Damn it. "So what you're telling me is that I've got a slacker with temper issues that can skate, but because I don't have a pair of cannons strapped to my chest, I'm shit out of luck?"

"Kinda what it sounds like. Sorry, girl."

I sighed. "That's okay. I'll just make the best of things. I mean, if I work my tail off, the show can't blame me, right?"

"I have no idea. Sorry. I've never been on TV. I'm a pre-med student, remember?"

I remembered. And groaned. "Why couldn't I have gotten a decent partner? All the guys got good ones. It's so unfair."

"Just do your best," Naomi said cheerfully. "That's all you can do."

A loud "*What the fuck?*" came from the other room.

Naomi paused. "What was that?"

"You heard that?" I cocked my free ear, listening to the other room. Bottles clinked with rapidity, and and then I heard what sounded like a lot of bottles shaking. "That would be my roommate, Prince Charming. Apparently they've decided that things will be more exciting if we're sharing a house together."

Naomi gasped, the sound tinny on the other end of the line. "You have to share a house with him? Are you freaking out?"

"Nope. Too many cameras around for him to try any shenanigans. He's here for PR. He'll be on his best behavior." I thought for a moment, and then added, "Theoretically."

I heard stomping, and then someone banged on my door, a crude version of a knock. "Hey. Hey! Mouthy girl. Open up."

I frowned at my closed door. The entire thing had vibrated when he'd knocked. It was just cheap wood, but still. I didn't want him destroying my room. I had to live here for the next two months, after all. "I'd better let you go, Naomi. Talk to you later."

"Good luck." She sounded worried. "You're going to need it. Break a leg."

"You don't tell a skater that," I yelped at her, but it ended up being the dial tone. Damn it! I could practically feel the juju going south on me. I went immediately to my desk and touched each of my lucky talismans in a row, trying to reverse the negativity.

Skaters were superstitious. I was more superstitious than most, but I also didn't like to take a chance on something like bad energy. I needed all my luck around me for the next two months.

Ty banged on my door again, and I set my phone down and went to answer it. I'd kept the door shut all afternoon, needing to unwind from the horrible meeting. One of the cameramen told me that we could be filmed anywhere in the house except for in our bedrooms, so I'd more or less hidden there. Like a coward. But I didn't have to be 'on' until tomorrow morning, so I'd save my mental fortitude for then. I had a feeling I'd need every ounce of patience possible.

I opened my door and a crack and gave Ty a cross look. "There a problem?" Sure enough, there was a camera hovering over his shoulder.

He looked pissed. His eyes were narrowed and he held a bottle of beer in his hand. Likely a warm beer. "Yeah, there's a problem. What did you do?"

"Do?" I blinked my eyes innocently.

"My beer's hot. The entire fridge is fucked. What did you do?"

I ignored the question he asked me and posed one of my own. "You're an athlete, right? You shouldn't drink beer if you want to remain in top form."

"I'm an athlete on hiatus stuck on a dumbass dancing show," he told me, his eyes narrowed. "What did you do to my fridge?"

"Ice skating, not dancing," I hissed at him. "And it's still a sport."

"Yeah. Okay." He was clearly humoring me. He jiggled the beer in front of my face. "All I want to know is if you're responsible for this."

I eyed it, and then his angry Neanderthal face. Did I think his nose had been broken only twice? I'd probably sorely underestimated. And right now? I couldn't blame those people that broke his nose. Heck, I'd be volunteering for a swipe right now myself. "If you're going to be an athlete," I told him, "act like one."

His mouth tightened with fury. "So it was you—"

I slammed my door shut in his face.

Silence. I cringed, expecting to hear a roar of rage. Maybe he'd scream names at me through the door. Something. He didn't seem like the type that could hold his temper. And they were filming, which wasn't great.

"You and I need to have a talk," he said through the door.

I ignored him.

"Fine then," he said after a long, long moment, voice surprisingly calm. "You've got to come out of there sometime to eat."

I sat down on my bed, cross legged, and pulled a box of organic granola bars off of my nightstand. I peeled one open and began to eat. I actually didn't have to leave my room. My bathroom was attached to my bedroom, and I'd brought in bottles of water and snacks so I could deliberately hide away all evening. I peeled a bar open, feeling pretty pleased with myself.

"So you ignoring me?" he asked.

I said nothing. He wanted to be childish? I could be childish too. Just watch me.

"All right then. Since you don't plan on answering, or coming out so we can talk about this shit, I'll just use your fridge. Problem solved."

I made a face at the door as he stomped away. It was going to be a long eight weeks.

THE NEXT MORNING, I WOKE UP AT 5 AM AND SHOWERED, READY TO face the day. Not only ready, but excited. This was my first day back being a professional, and I was determined to show my stuff.

I dressed in a red leotard and black tights, yanked my hair into my bun, and grabbed my lucky socks. My skates were pulled off of their hook and slung over my shoulder, I touched my talismans laid out on my desk, and then I was ready to go. Sucking in a breath, I cracked my door open, peeking out.

Nothing.

I stepped out of the bedroom and glanced around. Everything seemed quiet. Ty's door was shut, so I didn't know if he was awake or not. My guess was 'not.' I turned the corner to the kitchen…and paused.

That *asshole.*

All the food that had been in my fridge was now strewn on the counters. Organic skim milk had been left out overnight to spoil, as had my tofu. My fruits, my organic juices, and my vegetables were strewn carelessly all over the counter as if they were just garbage in the way.

Bottles of beer lined the countertops, along with discarded bottle tops and empty bags of potato chips. Good lord. The man had himself a bacchanal-for-one last night. I moved across the garbage-strewn kitchen and peeked inside my fridge. Sure enough, it was crammed full of his beer and a leftover pizza delivery box. I slammed it shut.

Furious, I grabbed fruits and vegetables from the counter, washed them, and shoved them into the Vitamix blender, thinking evil thoughts about my partner. I added ice and turned it on viciously, hoping the sound woke him up, and then poured my fruit-and-spinach smoothie into a tall bottle and took it with me out to the rink.

It was bright outside despite the early hour, and birds were chirping in the trees. All in all, not a bad day so far. I was determined to make this work, too. The thought of getting back on the ice in a professional capacity—and not in a dinosaur costume—excited me. I'd show the network who was dedicated and willing to go the extra mile on this team. It didn't matter if Ty Randall sucked as a partner. I'd be so amazing that it wouldn't matter. And maybe Svetlana would stay home with her baby. Maybe.

I pushed open the door to the rink and inhaled at the delicious scent of fresh ice that met my nose. Perfect, just perfect. I moved to the side of the rink and sat down on one of the benches, then began to carefully check my skates over before I began warm-ups.

Ice skates were important to a skater—they were the most important piece of equipment, actually, if one ignored the ice itself and the need for strong muscles, long hours of practice, and lots of determination. Like dancers, we babied—and personalized—our skates. Mine were white leather, beaten up to suppleness. They fit perfectly, the ankles tight enough to grip but flexible enough to allow good movement. My blades were razor sharp, as always, and I checked my laces, and then flipped over my skate and touched the talismans I had duct-taped to the bottom. My lucky penny, two fortune-cookie slips that had promised good things, a sequin from every costume I'd worn in competition, and a sticker of a pink lucky rabbit's foot from Naomi. She'd wanted to give me a real rabbit's foot for luck, but this was better because it would be on my feet. Satisfied everything was in place, I laced my skates up tight, downed the rest of my breakfast, removed the guards from my blades, and then approached the ice.

I have an entire routine of mojo-producing things, but my favorite is to kiss the ice before I step onto it. It was something I started to do when I was a child, and it's always brought me luck. Even after years of skating, I hadn't changed. Kissing the ice was like asking it for permission. It showed respect, and it gave good juju.

I was a big fan of juju.

So I leaned in and kissed the ice, inhaling the crisp scent of it. God, I loved the ice. Nothing made me happier. The ritual done, I got back to my feet and set my skates on it, testing the feel. Somebody must have come by and ran a Zamboni overnight, because the ice was slick and spotless, not carved up in the slightest. I began to skate along the edges of the rink in circles, warming up my muscles while tearing up the ice just a little to make it easier to skate on.

Wouldn't want precious Ty Randall falling and breaking his nose again, would we?

Once I was sufficiently warmed up, I began to work up a sweat, going through moves just to get my muscles going. An axel on this round, then a double axel. When I was fully warmed up, I'd do a triple. I also practiced my toe loops and a triple lutz. Then a sit spin, and moved into a standing spin, grasping my leg and pulling it high over my head to form a clean line.

The door to the gym opened, and I broke out of the spin and circled back around, hissing to a stop at the sight of an unfamiliar woman. I frowned, glancing around. "This is a private rink."

"I'm Imelda Garcia," she told me in a pleasant voice. "Your assigned choreographer."

Oh. Disappointment flashed through me. She…didn't look like what I'd pictured. I skated to the edge of the ice, and then dug my toe pick in to stop in place. "Hi. I'm Zara."

She chuckled, looking for all the world like a schoolteacher more than a choreographer. Her hair was short and feathered with gray, and she wore a yellow cardigan and a pair of navy slacks with her loafers. She carried a big bag over one shoulder that didn't look like athletic gear. "I know who you are. Now, where's your partner?"

I skated away, keeping my muscles warm. "No clue. Sleeping off his beer, I suppose."

She frowned at me. "You haven't seen him? It's nine in the morning."

"Is it?" I hadn't noticed. I'd been so caught up in enjoying my skating— my own private rink!—that I had lost track of time. I'd been picturing routines in my head, trying to think of the best moves that would be easy enough for a douchebag like Ty to do and still have us come out looking great.

"Yes. Where's your cameraman?"

"I don't know that either," I told her, shrugging. Then, I curled into another sit spin, because skating was easier than answering questions. A freaking choreographer. Imelda was nice, but I resented that we had to have one. I liked to do my own routines, damn it. Wouldn't I know what was best for me? This was like having a coach again—worse, because at least a coach would be positive and encourage you. A coach could tell you how to fix your moves.

Imelda didn't look as if she'd ever stepped onto the ice. I gave her another wary look as I circled around, hands on my hips. She had a phone out and was calling someone. A minute later, she put it down and gave me a tight smile. "We'll get this taken care of."

"Okay," I told her, and I began to speed around the ice, jumping into a triple Salchow. I was off, though, and doubled it. Damn it. I lifted my skate and rubbed the penny taped to the bottom for more good juju, then skated around to try again. Nailed it the second time.

I was still skating and being ignored by Imelda when the double doors of the ice rink opened a short time later. In walked Ty, dressed in sweats and a dirty wife-beater. His eyes were puffy slits that told me he was hung over, and his feet were bare. Lovely. At his side, another man in an ugly striped polo shirt and khakis talked into his phone, a frown on his face. He held a pair of skates out to Ty, who snatched them with a grumpy look.

Ty had the look of a kid that had been called to the principal's office.

Damn. I couldn't even enjoy that. It had to be embarrassing. Who was that guy? His dad? His manager? It didn't matter. Ty being schooled in front of me like a child wouldn't do much for his mood.

The man clicked his phone shut and turned to Ty. He pointed at the ice. "Now. You're here, and you're going to do this competition like we talked about. If you ever want to fight in Vegas again, you need to take this shit seriously. Show people you have a heart. Because if you don't, you're finished. Remember Mike Tyson? The only reason he ever got work in this town again is because he had good PR people."

Ty rolled his eyes and his shoulders slouched, the very picture of irritated sulking. "You know I don't want to do this, Chuck."

"Do you trust me?"

Ty glanced over at me, as if to say, "Do you believe this shit?" He smacked his lips a few times, as if considering, and then let his shoulders drop again. "Yeah."

"Then no more fucking beer orgies. You're going to shut up, and pay attention, and if you value your career, you're going to do this fucking dancing shit, understand me?"

"Ice skating," I corrected.

"Ice dancing," Imelda said. "You're both right."

"Actually, it's really not ice dancing," I began, and then stopped. Oh, whatever. No one was listening anyhow. I twirled on the ice slowly, watching the scene play out.

There was another long, tense pause. Then Ty moved forward and sat down on the bench, putting his skates on. Once they were laced, he looked at his manager, then at me, and stepped onto the ice.

"Okay," his manager said. "Why don't you show them what you can do."

Ty glanced over at him and took a few shuffling steps onto the ice, spreading his hands. "Voila."

"I know you can skate," I told him. "Don't pull this shit." And I circled around him just to show off.

He smirked at me and turned around, skating backward now. So I did another circle and passed him, just to show my stuff. The next few minutes turned into a pissing war between us. The faster he skated, the faster I moved around him, determined to zigzag in front every chance I got.

Then, when I crossed over in front of him again, he grabbed me around the waist and twirled us both in a circle, my skates flying into the air.

I yelped in surprise.

He laughed and looked over at Imelda. "Well, at least she's easy to lift."

I squirmed out of his grasp, flustered. That contact had felt weirdly intimate. I mean, it wasn't as if I didn't expect to be grabbed on the ice. I did. That was how lifts happened. But that spontaneous embrace? That flustered me.

Imelda got to her feet and held out two pieces of paper in front of us. "Now that you two are warmed up, I thought I'd go over the choreography for the first routine."

I skidded away from Ty on the ice and moved to the edge, reaching out and grabbing the first piece of paper from Imelda. "Print outs? Really?"

"So you can learn your steps," she told me in a calm voice. "I've already mapped out your routine and what you'll be wearing."

"You what?" I looked at her in shock. "You picked music and every-thing?"

"I have. It's all taken care of."

That…didn't make me happy. "So why did you guys get professional figure skaters?"

She tilted her head at me. "What do you mean?"

I shook the printout at her. "You can get any idiot to do a jump and a sit spin. After all, you're having celebrities do this."

"Hey," Ty said sharply.

"It's true," I said, looking down the list and reading it. "This is kiddie shit. So if you're picking out the routines and the costumes and the music, why not hire amateurs? Why do you want real skaters doing this?" I was lashing out at her, but I was growing increasingly disappointed with this job. I thought it would be a chance for me to show my stuff in a public venue. Get my face back on the map. Instead, they wanted an idiot that would just wander around the ice and do what she was told.

I scanned the routine she'd made for us. Yawn city. This was turning into a disappointing job, all right. I'd be paid well, but that was about it. No one would be interested in a figure skater who did as shitty a routine as what Imelda had mapped out. I'd get a paycheck for this job and not much more.

To say I was frustrated was an understatement.

Imelda looked clearly hurt by my arguments. "Well, Miss Zara, I understand your concerns. Would you like for me to tell the network that you're not interested in doing the routine?"

I blinked a few times. "No, ma'am. I want this job."

She beamed at me, just as if I hadn't argued with her at all. "Well then, I believe we should practice, don't you? Now for starters, let's get you two comfortable with each other. You both look like two porcupines with how prickly you're being to one another." She gestured with her hands for us to move forward. "Ice dancing is all about body language, and right now your body language is telling me 'no thank you.' I want you both to pull in together and try to waltz on the ice."

I dug my toe pick into the ice and skated toward Ty, extending my hand for him to take.

He grasped it in his, and I was immediately struck at how strong—and big—his hand was compared to mine. I knew that my build was small, but standing next to Ty's bulk, he made me feel positively dwarfed. His big hand clutched mine, and his hand went to my waist, pulling me in.

Did I think that Ty spontaneously holding my hands had been intimate? It was nothing compared to him putting his hand at my waist and dragging me against him. My breast pressed against his chest, and my body fitted against his.

Imelda tittered. "Not that close. This isn't dirty dancing."

"Yeah, that'd probably get better ratings," Ty muttered, his gaze flicking to me.

I smothered a laugh. "This is serious," I told him in a stern voice. "Please concentrate."

"Further apart, please," Imelda instructed us.

I obediently took a step backward, extending our embrace outward.

Imelda continued to sit on her bench, directing us from afar as she guided us on our posture. She never took a step toward the ice, content with politely barking orders from afar as we shuffled, clasped hands, re-clasped, adjusted our arms, and whatever else she wanted us to do. When she was satisfied with our posture, we were instructed to simply dance around the rink in time.

I picked it up easily, which was no surprise, since I had a lot of skating experience.

Ty was definitely the weak link on our team. He struggled to find a rhythm, and his hand clasped mine so tightly that it was sweating. He frowned the entire time, watching our feet. When he stumbled, he thrust me away from him, clearly done. "This is stupid. I hate this."

"Ty," his manager said warningly.

"I feel like I'm fucking back in high school," Ty muttered.

"You're acting like it too," I told him in a light voice, extending my hand back out to him.

He glared at me, wiping sweat from his brow. "Aren't you tired? Don't you want a break? I think we've got this."

"Actually," I told him. "We don't have this. We're not even close to having this. Your steps aren't even remotely close to being in time with mine, your arms aren't locked, and your skating has no rhythm at all. If we go out there like this, you'll make us a laughingstock, and I'm not about to have that happen. So if it takes twelve hours for us to get down how to move around on the ice? I'm fine with that, and you should be, too. Understand?"

He pushed my extended hand away. "I'm not doing this for twelve more hours today."

"Fine then," I told him. "You can take the rest of the day off, and we'll do twelve hours tomorrow of nothing but holding hands and skating together."

He threw his hands up, as if done. "You know what? I'm out of here. Close enough. We have two weeks to learn this shit." He began to skate off of the ice.

I skated after him. "You can't quit. It's barely even eleven am. That's way too early to finish for the day."

Both Imelda and his manager were frowning at him. "Ty," his manager began.

"Nope," Ty said, stomping onto the carpeted steps with his skates, and then outside, not even bothering to take his skates off. "Done," he yelled. "I've done enough."

I put my hands on my hips, frustrated. "Well, what the hell?" I looked over at Ty's manager. "Are you going to let him just walk away like that?"

He shrugged. "I can't stop him. It doesn't matter if he looks like he can skate, missy. The important thing is that he's on the show and the public likes what they see enough to forget about any…indiscretions."

Unreal. So Ty was going to get to do whatever he wanted, and I was the one whose career was going to be sabotaged?

This was so freaking unfair.

Chapter Four

Zara? She's a real piece of work. When she's not nagging me—constantly, I might add—she's at work on the ice. Body of a twig, heart of a champion. Gotta admire that. —Ty Randall, Day Two of Preliminary Practice, Ice Dancing with the Stars

I CONTINUED TO SKATE SOLO FOR THE REST OF THE AFTERNOON, learning the steps and beats of the routine as best as I could without a partner at my side. After all, just because he was lazy didn't mean I was. Imelda hadn't provided the music yet, but I didn't need it. A good skater learned the routine first and meshed it with the music later. At least, that was how I'd always been taught. I wasn't sure if it would work as well with 'ice dancing' (or whatever we were calling the skating we were doing), but I'd probably find out soon enough.

By the time I was satisfied with the amount of work I'd put in, it was getting late, and the sun was going down. I'd worked up an exhausting sweat, my leotard soaked. But I felt good. My muscles were loose and aching from the workout I'd put them through, and my mood was awesome despite my terrible partner. I had a real skating job again, despite the crap partner and kiddie routine.

They wanted a mannequin that would go out on the ice and do their rinky-dink performance? I'd be the best damn mannequin on ice ever.

(I mean, after all, I'd already been a pink dinosaur on ice. A mannequin was a step up.)

I took a long, hot shower in the locker room after practice. It was a little unnerving to notice that the gym had only one shower in the adjoining locker rooms, but I guessed it wouldn't matter since Ty didn't intend to work up much of a sweat. I changed into leggings and a tank top, grabbed my skates and dirty laundry, and headed back to the cottage.

When I stepped inside, it was dark. Flashes of light came from the living room, along with the sounds from a loud action movie. Figured. He was watching TV while I was skating and learning our routine. Rolling my eyes, I dumped my stuff in my room and then considered a moment longer.

I could let this continue, or I could nip it in the bud and have a talk with my partner.

I went for option B.

Heading into the living room of our cottage, I spotted Ty sprawled low on the overstuffed leather sofa. His legs were kicked up onto the art deco coffee table, the remote in one hand, beer in the other. A scatter of empty beer bottles covered the rest of the coffee table.

I crossed the room and sat down on the far end of the couch, away from him, and folded my legs up against me, hugging one knee. I waited for him to say something to me.

He didn't blink an eye, just continued watching TV. After a moment, he lifted his beer to his lips and took another long swig.

"Are you a drunk?" I asked.

"Only when I'm imprisoned," he said in a flat voice, gaze still glued to the television.

"This isn't a prison," I told him. "This is supposed to be your second chance. And it's not going to work if you're cutting out early every day just to drink."

He looked over at me, then, and studied my face for a long moment. After a beat, he offered his beer to me. "You sound like you could use a drink."

I rolled my eyes. "Whatever."

"You scared?" He wiggled his eyebrows at me. "These are healthy. All those grains and all."

Sighing, I snatched the beer from his hand and took a gigantic swig. I could never ignore a challenge. Almost immediately, I began to cough and choke. The taste was…vile.

He snickered. "Is that your first beer, little girl?"

"No," I lied. Okay, so maybe it was. I wasn't exactly a party girl. The closest I'd ever gotten to 'party' was champagne on New Year's Eve. "God, that tastes awful."

"Take another sip. It'll get better." He grinned lazily at me.

I took another sip and made a face. Still awful. I handed it back. "How can you drink that?"

"Like I said, I'm imprisoned." He took the bottle back and swigged it as if it were nothing. "Imprisoned and my cellmate's an uptight stick with a mouth."

I bristled. A stick with a mouth? "Fuck you, Randall. I was coming out here to bury the hatchet, but I don't care if you flame out and embarrass yourself on national television. You're a huge jackass."

"Stick with a *big* mouth," he muttered to himself, and took another sip of beer.

I flounced up from the couch. "You'd better be there at practice tomorrow. That's all I'm saying. I am not going to let you ruin my career just because you're too macho to learn a few skate routines. Understand me? Because if you think you're hated by the public now? You just wait. I can give them all kinds of shit to film in the next two weeks that will completely decimate what's left of your image. If you tank my career, I'm dragging you down with me."

And with that, I stormed to my room.

THAT NIGHT, I WAS HAVING THE DIRTIEST DREAM.

"Hey baby," Ty Randall breathed into my ear. "Move your hands, sweetheart." His big body pressed up against mine, and he felt delicious. We were on the ice in sparkling white costumes, waiting for the music to start. He'd pulled my entire body against his, and our legs were intertwined in a gravity-defying lock that was only possible in dreams. His legs rubbed against my own, so big and strong. His arm went over my shoulders and pulled me against him even more, and I was deliciously enveloped against his chest.

How had he known exactly what I wanted? Ty Randall, all over me.

One hand pushed onto my breast and I frowned down at it. I was pretty sure the judges would count off for groping during a routine. He squeezed…

And my eyes flew open.

We weren't on the ice.

I wasn't alone in bed.

A big, warm male body was pressed against my own, his legs mixed with mine. Ty Randall had me pulled against his much bigger body, and his hand really was on my breast, kneading it. He was under the covers with me.

I flung his hand off of me and sat up, horrified. Horrified at him, and horrified at my own reaction (which wasn't *all* rage). "What are you doing?"

He didn't open his eyes, simply burrowed deeper into my pillows. "Sleeping."

"No! You can't sleep in here! What are you doing in my *room*, you idiot?"

He mumbled something that sounded like 'I'm the celebrity and I should get whatever room I want'.

I jabbed him with my finger and looked over at the clock. 5:55 in the morning. Five minutes before my alarm was set to go off. "You can't have whatever room you want. I'm in this one. I gave you the big one *because* you're the celebrity!"

"Windows," he mumbled into my pillow. "Want the one without the windows. Hurts my head."

Oh, he wanted his head to hurt, did he? I leaned into his ear. "FUCK YOUR HEAD. GET OUT OF MY BED."

He groaned and jerked upright, knocking his skull into my nose.

I gasped, flying backward, my fingers clutched to my nostrils. Blood was suddenly gushing from my nose. "Fuck!"

He was instantly awake, sitting up in the bed. His hand clutched his head. "Oh shit. You okay?"

I ran to my bathroom, flicking the light on and reaching for a towel, not answering him. Blood was everywhere.

"Shit. Shit shit shit," he moaned. I heard the bed creak even as I pressed the towel to my nose, waiting for it to stop bleeding. "Fuck, Zorba, I'm sorry."

"*Zara*," I told him, my voice muffled from the towel.

"Zara," he echoed. "Zara. Zara. Sorry. I didn't mean to bloody your nose." Ty gave me a chagrined look. There were dark rings under his eyes, and he looked like a mess. "You just startled the hell out of me when you yelled in my ear."

I shot him the bird, still pressing the towel to my nose with my other hand. "I'm going to have two black eyes now, thanks to you."

"Ah fuck," he rubbed a hand down his face. "Great. Now I'm going to have the reputation of beating up girls as well as biting noses."

"I'm not a girl, remember? I'm just a stick with a mouth," I said bitterly.

"Actually, I felt your tits. They're pretty good, given that you look like you're fourteen."

"Fuck you! I'm twenty-five!"

"I know, I know." He raised his hands in the air, apology on his rough features. "Can we talk about this, Zara? Come to a compromise?"

"You're not getting my room!"

He looked confused for a moment, and then rubbed a hand down his face. "Not that. I don't give a shit about that now. But if my manager sees you with two black eyes and the camera crew films that? I'm done. I'm so done. Here." He shoved my makeup bag at me. "Put some powder or girl shit on it and cover it up."

"No. I'm going to tell everyone you head butted me." I'd just leave out the part where it was an accident. "At least this way, I can salvage my career."

"It would totally fuck me. Come on, Zara, please." He dropped to his knees, and I realized for the first time that he was wearing a pair of boxer briefs and nothing else. His big, muscular body flexed as he clasped his meaty hands in front of him in a supplicating pose. And his thighs? When he knelt, his thighs were nothing but enormous cords of muscle. The athlete in me really liked that. Far too much.

"Look," he said, giving me a sincere expression of misery. "This is me, begging you for mercy. It'll totally screw me over if they think I hit you on purpose. After my last incident, no one will think it's an accident."

"Well, we can just tell them the truth," I said, too-sweetly. "I'll just say that you got totally plastered and crawled into my bed, and when I tried to get away from you, you head butted me."

He groaned, covering his face with his hands. "I am so fucking screwed."

"Unless…" I teased, checking the washcloth and turning it. Still bleeding. Ugh. He'd smacked me good.

Ty looked up at me with so much hope in his eyes that I felt a twinge of pity for the guy. I knew what it was like to fuck up and have everything come crashing down around you. Also, his big pale eyes were kind of sexy. Silvery, almost. Normally they made him look mean, but right now? I kind of liked it.

"Unless you promise to take this whole ice dancing thing seriously," I told him, pulling the wad of fabric away from my nose and checking my face in the mirror. My normally tiny nose looked like a potato, and my eyes were already swelling. Lovely. The bleeding had mostly stopped, though, and I looked over at Ty. "I will go out there and tell everyone I practiced late. No, that *we* practiced late. You had a change of heart and came back. My toe pick got caught on something, and I miscalculated and landed on my face."

Hope lit up his brutish features, and for the first time since I'd met him, Ty didn't seem like a Neanderthal or a caveman. He was actually kind of cute when he wasn't scowling or drunk. His face was a little more rugged than I liked normally, and he'd definitely taken several hard punches to the face, but he had an appeal to him when he was looking up at me like that. "You'd do that for me? Lie to everyone?"

"I will…*if*," I said, and I made sure to emphasize the 'if.' "*If* you take this seriously."

He considered me for a long, long moment, those silver eyes regarding my face. "How seriously?"

"You know what? Never mind—"

"I'm kidding, I'm kidding." Ty got up from his knees and grabbed my arms when I turned away. "You mean the dancing shit, right? Fine, fine. I'll go to practice."

"No, you'll go to practice early and you'll stay late," I corrected. "Just like me. And I'll go on and on about how nice of a partner you are, and how sweet and caring. And you're going to work your tail off for this and make us both look good. It's not just your career on the line here, buddy. It's mine, too. If I don't look good this season I won't get asked back again."

"No sequins?" He looked dubious. "I really, really refuse to wear sequins."

"What is it with you and sequins?" I gave him an exasperated look. "No embarrassing costumes for either of us. We both take this seriously and come out of this to fix our careers, okay? All I want from you is that you work hard and don't quit."

"I can do that," he said, sincerity on his face. "I promise."

"And no more beer," I added.

"That's two things."

I put my hands on my hips and glared at him.

"Fine." He sighed. "Wasn't going to drink any more after this, anyhow. I think I'm scared straight."

"Good. So we both agree to work our asses off and do whatever it takes to fix our careers?"

Ty nodded at me. "Agreed."

I spit on my palm and held it out to him. "Shake on it."

He looked at me like I'd just grown another head. "I'm not touching your hand if you spit on it."

I jiggled it at him. "You can't seal a deal otherwise. It won't work. The juju won't be there."

His lip curled as if in disgust, and he stared at me for a moment longer. Was the big MMA fighter squeamish?

I waited, staring at him, hand still extended.

He sighed, spit into his own hand, and then smacked it against mine. "You are a strange chick," he told me. And then he pulled his hand from mine and washed it off quickly.

I cleaned off my own hand and then dabbed at my nose one more time. It looked awful. I was going to look horrible for the next week on camera. Lucky me.

"All right," he told me. "Let's just forget about this and go back to bed."

As if on cue, my alarm clock began to beep. I gave him a wry look and headed to the side of the bed, clicking off the alarm. "No sleep. It's time to get up and train."

He gave me a withering look.

WE MET FIFTEEN MINUTES LATER. I WAS DRESSED IN MY TYPICAL leotard and tights (hey, everyone has a work uniform), and my hair was pulled back in my standard bun. I hadn't bothered with makeup for my nose and swelling eyes. Instead, I'd put a dainty pink bandaid, which matched my leotard, over my nose and pulled on my lucky socks that I'd washed in the sink the night before.

Then, skates in hand, I headed out to the rink to warm up.

To my surprise (and pleasure), Ty was there, lacing up his skates as he sat on the bench. Good. So he was going to take this seriously. I sat next to him and flipped over my skates, mentally assessing all of my luck charms taped to the bottom of my skates as I touched each one in order.

He leaned over and glanced at my skate. "What's all that shit?"

"They're for good luck." I pulled my skate away protectively, and then began to put it on. First the left skate, because that was the lucky one. You never started with your right foot.

Ty grunted. "You superstitious?"

"No more than anyone else," I told him, tightening the laces on my skate until I was pleased with how it felt. Then, I gave it a wiggle and moved to the other skate. A few minutes later, I was good, and I took off my blade guards, and then headed to the ice. As was my custom, I leaned over the ice and gave it a kiss.

Behind me, Ty snorted. "Did you just kiss the ice?"

"Good luck," I told him. "We don't want any bad juju."

"Uh huh," he said skeptically. "You should try making your own luck for a change."

"You should shut your mouth," I said pleasantly, getting back to my feet and stepping onto the ice. It was like welcoming a lover—not that I'd ever done that, either. I sighed with pure pleasure as my skates glided onto the ice, and I closed my eyes, rolling my shoulders and working out the kinks in my neck. No sign of our cameraman yet, or Imelda. It was just the two of us.

I began to skate slowly around the ice, warming up and shaking out my muscles. As a test, I swung around and popped into a double axel. Smooth and flawless. Nice. I continued to warm up, adding the occasional jump just for fun. Nothing hard, nothing strenuous, just prepping my body for a long workout ahead.

Still, when Ty skated close to me and began to keep pace with my strides, he looked pretty impressed. "You're good."

I gave him a funny look. "I know I'm good. That was just warm-ups, though."

"You were in the Olympics?"

I nodded, and then flipped around to skate backward so I wouldn't have to answer more questions.

He wouldn't be deterred, though. Ty followed my lead and turned as well, skating into a tight edge and showing more agility on the ice than I'd given him credit for. He caught up to me and started again. "You get any medals?"

"I don't want to talk about the Olympics," I told him.

"Why not? You talk about everything else. Half the time you won't shut up."

I skidded to a halt, jamming my toe-pick into the ice. My hands went to my hips. "Have I asked you what it feels like to chew off some guy's nose?"

He scowled at me, his mood going dark right away.

"Exactly. You don't ask me about the Olympics, and I won't ask you about eating some guy's face."

"Fine," he said in a curt voice.

"Fine," I said, keeping my own tone light. I was going to be nice if it killed me. I dropped into a loose sit spin to end the conversation.

When I was sufficiently warmed up, I skated toward Ty. Hopefully he'd had time to cool down a bit. "So do you want to practice ice waltzing until Imelda gets here?"

He wiped his hands on his sweatpants, and held them out to me. "Sure. Let's go for it."

I placed his hand at my waist like we'd been shown and flushed, remembering that I'd woke up that morning with his hand on my breast. *Don't think about that, Zara*, I scolded myself. I took his other hand and clasped it in mine, then put my other on his shoulder. I looked into his eyes. Despite all we'd been through in the last two days, our embrace still felt intimate as heck, and my body reacted, my skin tingling as I became aware of him close to me. I needed to get used to a partner, or this was going to make me flustered and nervous every time he touched me. I glanced at him, and he was staring at my face with intensity.

"Damn, you look like hell," he said, shaking his head. "Your nose is swelled up like a strawberry."

"Just *dance*." I bit the two words out, any attraction I might have felt toward him disappearing in an instant.

We practiced keeping in time with each other. Ty was a big guy, and I was a lot smaller than him, so we spent a lot of time matching our strides. I had to lengthen mine while still seeming graceful, and he had to manage to somehow not mince while keeping in time with me. It wasn't easy. We were starting to get into a rhythm, though, and by the time it was nine in the morning, we were moving around the ice in a reasonable facsimile of partnership.

The door to our rink opened, and we both glanced over. Imelda, the camera crew, Ty's manager, and two other people I didn't recognize all stood there.

The cavalry had arrived. Fun. And they were all staring at my face with horror. I felt Ty tense up, his hands still clasping me close. He was trying, though, and because he was holding up his end of the deal, I'd hold up mine.

I patted Ty's arm. "Let me handle this." I pulled away from him and skated to the edge of the ice. "Morning," I said in my most cheerful voice. "I was wondering if you guys would ever get here."

The cameras immediately hovered around me, filming my brutally awful face at every angle. I couldn't say I blamed them. Imelda moved to the edge of the ice and put her hands on my chin in a motherly way. "Poor Zara. What happened to your face?"

"Oh, that." I waved a hand casually. "I was practicing late last night, and I guess I was more tired than I thought. I went to stop on my toe pick, but it wasn't sharp enough and I miscalculated." I smacked my hands together. "Boom, flat on the ice. Luckily, Ty was there to pick me up. He offered to take me to the emergency room but I figured it was just a little bump." I touched the pink Band-Aid on my nose innocently. "Does it look bad?"

Imelda was giving Ty a skeptical look. She glanced at him and back at me, and I knew what she was thinking. Did the big, mean MMA fighter beat up on fragile little Zara Pritchard? "He came back to skate last night?" Imelda asked skeptically. At her side, Ty's coach took one look at me and stalked toward his client, practically vibrating with fury.

"He did," I said brightly, glancing back at Ty so he could back up my story. "We had a little chat last night, and he wanted to come back out and practice some more, so we did. We're getting better, too. Did you want to see what we've been practicing?"

Ty's manager looked at my swollen face, then back to Ty. Then back to me. "You said this wasn't him? You swear?"

I blinked my puffy eyes in what I hoped was an innocent expression and not something hideous. "No. Ty's been the perfect gentleman. Why would you think he'd hurt me?"

He looked back at Ty. "That wasn't you?"

Ty crossed his arms over his chest, tucking his hands into his armpits. He forced a casual stance, though I could still see him practically vibrating with tension. "It wasn't me, man. Chill."

"I told him you'd all say that," I exclaimed, and gave a fake laugh. "No, it was just me getting too ahead of my own feet. It'll go away in time for the show." And I skated back to Ty's side as if that settled things and we were bestest buddies.

No one said anything for a long moment, and I pretended to check the laces on my shoes, waiting. Waiting for someone to call bullshit on us. Waiting for someone to tear into Ty.

"Oh. Well, okay then," Imelda said. "Let's get your measurements."

I stood back up, looking at Imelda with a question in my eyes. "Measurements?"

The two strangers moved forward, pulling out measuring tapes and sewing implements. "For this week's costumes," one of them said.

"No sequins," Ty immediately called out.

One of them looked up and wrote that down. "What about you, Miss Pritchard? Sequins?"

"I don't care. So what are we wearing?" I skated over and tried to get a glimpse at the clipboard that one of the costumers was carrying.

"The theme for this first week is country," Imelda said.

I made a face and looked back at Ty, hoping he'd share my dismay. "Really? Country? How are we supposed to skate to wailing banjos?"

"I have music picked out," Imelda said. "And we're incorporating line dancing, so this should be fun."

I stared at her, an unpleasant look on my face. Line dancing? Fun? "We're not dancing to classical?" I'd always been skeptical of skaters who picked trendy music simply to get more of a rise from the audience. After all, in ice skating, the only ones you really had to impress were the judges' panel, and if you came out to rock and roll, there was always going to be someone that wasn't a fan. Classical music was safe.

"'Boot Scootin' Boogie,'" Imelda announced cheerfully. "The required elements this week are toe step sequences, so it'll be perfect."

"Toe step what?" Ty skated to my side and looked over at me. "What's she talking about? Required elements?"

I crossed my arms over my chest. "Every time you skate a routine, there are required elements that you have to perform to get a certain number of points. You can't just go out there and skate whatever you want."

He rubbed his shaved head. "I thought that was exactly what you did."

I laughed. "Uh, no. There are all kinds of specifics. And our judges are going to be other figure skaters, so we'll need to be as precise as possible."

"Precise as possible to 'Boot Scootin' Boogie?'"

I shrugged. I'd never even heard the song. "If it's what the network wants, it's what the network will get."

"Great," Imelda said. "I like to hear that."

"What size skate do you wear?" one of the costumers asked me, fingers poised over his iPad.

"Doesn't matter," I told him. "I'm using my skates. They're all broken in the way I like them."

He eyed my beaten-up, white leather skates. Then made a note on his iPad. "We'll make some skate covers attached to your tights."

"Fine by me." I stepped off of the ice and moved forward. Immediately, the one costume designer wrapped a tape around my thigh, measuring.

That was…weird. Normally female skaters just wore tights, and they didn't have to be measured to the extent that she was. "So what's with the thigh measurements?" I asked casually.

"For your chaps," the other said.

"Chaps?" Ty repeated. Then a low groan escaped his throat.

I shot him a deadly warning look. "Chaps are fine," I said, even though I thought they were stupid, especially for a skating costume.

"Chaps are fine," he repeated in a flat voice, his gaze on the pink Band-Aid on my nose.

I was glad he saw things my way.

Chapter Five

Chaps. Goddamn chaps. If there's sequins, I'm leaving.
—Ty Randall, to his manager

WE PRACTICED OUR "BOOT SCOOTIN'" ROUTINE DAILY, AND I GREW
to hate it a little more each time.

To be fair, though, Ty never complained. Perhaps it was the sight
of my swollen face that made him close-lipped, or the fact that I never
complained about Imelda's choices (poor choices, if you asked me) of what
we would do. It was like he'd drawn up his belt and decided to just endure.

Kind of like me.

The routine was child's play for me, but it was clear that it was tough for
Ty. For starters, he tended to surge while skating instead of gliding gracefully. I suspected that was a holdover from his years of hockey training, and
it took us days of simply holding each other in an ice dancing embrace
before we started to move together fluidly. Once we did, though, Ty gave
me a cocky little grin as if to say "See?"

Of course, then we added the music, and things went to hell all over
again.

I hated the song. Hated it. I loved classical music, and this piece was
the antithesis of that, all twanging vocals and guitars. Ty seemed to like it,

though, and I caught him humming it under his breath, as if the tune were still stuck in his head even when we were off the ice.

Which made sense, seeing as we've heard it so many times that I've been hearing the song in my dreams.

Ty worked hard, though. I had to give the guy credit. Once he'd decided that he was going to do this, he was as determined as I was. If I was there at six in the morning, so was he. If I stayed and skated until eight at night, so did he. He didn't get off the ice until I did, and I tended to work long hours. Not only because I wanted to get things just right, but because I truly loved being on the ice and pushing my body to the limit.

Too bad the routine wouldn't let me. While we practiced the simplistic step sequences over and over so Ty could get them right, I kept feeling the urge to add to the routine, to flick my skate in a showy fashion, or to add little twirls here and there that would make the program more artistic.

I had to constantly remind myself that I was just the mannequin. So I practiced smiling and looking like I was having a blast while I did Imelda's simplistic—and dare I say, boring—routine. And when we took breaks, I punched things up and added a few jumps just for fun, and just because I could.

Ty was taking a breather off to the side as we finished that day's practice. He watched me come down from a triple axel that was perfectly timed with the change in the music that led to the chorus, and gave me a funny look, wiping his sweat-covered brow. "That was awesome. Why can't we add that stuff in the routine?"

I skated back to him, ignoring the endless twang of the music. "I'd love to, but there are two problems."

"What's that?"

I shook out my legs, feeling the burn from the hours of practice. I was just as sweaty as he was—and about ready to call it a night. "Well, for one, Imelda would freak out, and she has the network's ear. I want to be seen as a team player, and changing the routine of the choreographer they selected for us? Not exactly a team-player move."

He grunted acknowledgment. "So what's the other problem?"

"The other is that you wouldn't be able to keep up," I said with a sly grin on my face. "I can do the hard shit. You can barely keep a clean edge."

He scowled at me, but I just grinned. We'd formed an easy sort of truce ever since he'd agreed to actually try to work, and we bickered and teased and were generally comfortable with each other. It wasn't quite friendship, but it wasn't out-and-out hatred, either.

"I could keep pace with you if I had enough practice," he told me arrogantly.

"No, you couldn't," I said, sauntering away, heading to the edge of the ice. "You'd need a lot of practice to even come close. And anyhow, I'm heading off to take a shower."

"Oh, no you don't," Ty said behind me, and I heard him skate closer. "I get the shower first."

"Nope," I said, skating a little faster. "You had it first yesterday." Out of all the money the network had spent, why only one damn shower at the ice rink? We fought over it every day.

"Oh yeah?" Ty's hands landed on my waist. He grabbed me and hauled me around, spinning me.

I shrieked with laughter as he spun me around once, and then flung me into the air. Was that supposed to scare me? I landed easily on my blade, with a flourish. "Was that what you call a partner toss? You'd better brush up."

"Yeah, but now you're further away from the bathroom," he told me, hopping off the ice and tossing on his blade guards. He sat down and began to quickly unlace his skates.

Damn it! I skated furiously over to the bench, snapped on my blade guards and then thumped down next to him, undoing my own laces. "You are not getting in there first," I hissed. "I got on the ice first this morning, so I get to the showers first! Those are the rules!"

"Those are stupid rules," he told me. "And your rules don't apply if I get in there first." He tugged at a knot on his skate.

Ha! I pulled mine off and tossed them aside, and then scooped up my towel and ran into the shower room. Success! It was all mine. I reached in to the shower compartment and turned it on, letting the water heat up. Then, I pulled my sweat-damp hair down from my bun and began to slide out of my leotard.

"Hey, thanks," Ty said in my ear. "You're heating up the water for me."

I gave a little scream and a jump, clutching my leotard to my front. One second later and I would have been topless. I turned away from him and glanced down at my front, making sure everything was covered. "What are you doing in here?"

"Gonna take my shower first, like I told you."

"I'm getting undressed," I protested.

"I'm already undressed," he told me, and a second later, I heard the sound of water splashing.

I turned around just in time to see a pair of beefy, pale buttocks disappear into the hot shower—my shower! My mouth went dry at the sight, though, and I stood there dumbly as he slid the glass enclosure door shut.

Holy shit. Ty Randall had just walked past me, naked, and I'd missed all the good parts.

The shower cracked open a moment later, and Ty stuck his head out, water streaming. "You're welcome to finish undressing and join me."

"You're dreaming!" I said quickly, and stormed out of there, feeling flustered as hell.

"I am," he called after me.

I WAS STILL FLUSTERED BY OUR CONVERSATION EVEN AFTER I RETREATED to my room and took a shower in my own small private bathroom. After I was clean, I opted to avoid the living room and kitchen a while longer and flopped down on my bed, my smartphone in hand, and began to Google him on the internet.

"Ty Randall bite" immediately pulled up dozens of search terms and videos. I clicked on the first video and began to watch.

Ty's rugged face filled my screen, his upper lip jutting. A moment later, he bared his teeth, revealing a bright blue mouth-guard. Oh, that was why his lip stuck out. He closed in on his opponent, dripping sweat, and began to fling punches at the guy while the other shielded his face. A moment later, the action reversed, and Ty was on the defensive. I watched every fist flung with brutal precision, wincing each time Ty took a smack to the face. That had to hurt, but Ty showed no emotion even as blood streamed down from his forehead. His opponent knocked his feet out from under him and then Ty was on the ground. A moment later, the opponent raised his foot and slammed Ty's thigh. Ouch. That looked like it hurt. And it seemed to enrage Ty, because he struggled his way back up a moment later and started to lay into his opponent. Right, left, right again, an uppercut, and then the guy went to the ground, and Ty locked him into a submission hold. The guy tapped out, and Ty was declared the winner.

But instead of taking his win and running with it, Ty attacked his opponent again, furious. He slammed the guy in the face with another round, and when the ref stepped in, Ty punched *him*. The audience roared in outrage, and Ty attacked his opponent again. Then, I saw it. Ty leaned in and bit the hell out of the guy's nose. When he pulled away, blood gushed from the other man's face and his opponent screamed, clawing his face. Ty spit out a wad of…something onto the mat, and the video cut away.

Dear *lord*.

I tried to rationalize what I'd just seen with the man I knew. Ty was a big, surly lug at times, but he was a hard worker and had never even come close to losing his cool with me. I knew he had the name of "Ty the MMA Biter" but I hadn't really registered what that meant until I'd seen the brutality for myself.

This was the man that was my partner? Me? With my fragile figure skater's form, five-foot-three height and hundred-and-two pound weight? No wonder they'd all freaked when they'd seen my swollen face. Of course, if they expected Ty not to play well with others, why cast him on the show?

Either he had friends at the network, or they wanted him to cause drama. I wondered if that was why they'd cast him with me, too.

THE NEXT DAY WAS THE LAST FULL PRACTICE DAY BEFORE THE LIVE show the next evening. I intended to spend the entire day on the ice with Ty, working on foot sequences. We had most of the routine down flat, but there was quick-stepping footwork in the chorus of the song, and Ty sometimes missed the beats. I couldn't blame him. It was like the routine went from childishly easy to moderate in the space of an instant, and my partner, who didn't have years of training, was struggling to keep up. He never complained though, just tried and tried again.

I was frustrated, but I think Ty was twice as frustrated as I was.

Sure enough, he was on the ice before me that morning. I did my usual luck routine, kissed the ice, and then stepped on, skating to warm up. It was clear Ty had already been there for some time, judging by the sweat on his brow.

"Hey," I told him, skating past.

"Hey," he said, barely glancing at me. His gaze was on his feet, and as I watched, he tried another shuffle step that still wasn't quite quick enough.

I winced. "You'll get it by tomorrow."

"Yeah," he said flatly.

I continued to skate, thinking of what I'd seen in the YouTube video last night. And what I'd seen as he'd stepped into the shower, too, as I skated past. A girl couldn't help but check a guy's ass out after she'd seen it naked. But my mind kept circling back to the fight and the vicious bite I'd seen.

"So," I started as I skated close.

He automatically took my hand, pulling me close into dancing position. "What's up?"

I put my hand in his, hesitating a moment. "I was just…you know, wondering."

"About?" He raised his scarred eyebrow at me, and I stared at it, momentarily fascinated. Was the scar from fighting?

"Um, your fight. What made you do it?"

"My fight?" He looked confused for a moment, still setting his hands in position.

"You know." I made a chomping motion with my teeth. "Your *fight*."

He snorted, the look on his face going shuttered. "Do we really need to talk about this right now?"

"I guess not," I said, though I was nosy and incredibly curious. And a little disappointed. We were friends, weren't we? Didn't friends talk with friends about this sort of thing? It must have been bad if they were making him come on the show when he was so vehemently opposed to it. Had the guy slept with Ty's girlfriend or something? Called his mom names? What? The curiosity was bothering me, but I tried to steer the conversation into safer subjects. "So, more dancing?"

"More dancing," he told me, sounding resigned. "For now."

"Oh?" I glanced around, but Imelda wasn't here, only our cameraman. "Where's our choreographer? For that matter, where's our costumes? Today was supposed to be dress rehearsal."

"Apparently there was an issue with the costume department because another team's costumes changed mid-week and had to be redone from scratch. That meant ours got delayed. Imelda ran off to go talk with the studio about it." He shrugged. "You really want her hanging around, criticizing our footwork?"

"Nah," I told him. "I just wanted to see what monstrosity she'd cooked up for us to wear. Most figure-skating costumes tend to be a bit on the flamboyant side, if you haven't noticed."

"Oh, I noticed," he said with a grin. "Which is why I always say—"

"—No sequins," I finished for him, laughing.

His eyes warmed and the grin spread wider. "Exactly. I'm telling you right now, though, if it looks Liberace-inspired, I'm not wearing it."

His smiles made me feel good. I placed my hand on his shoulder and told him, "If it's Liberace-inspired, I won't blame you."

Ty clicked a remote in his pocket, and the music began to play. We started the routine, and I began to count steps aloud to try and help him move along fast enough to keep up with the music. By the time the chorus rolled around, we were a step behind. He cursed. "This fucking footwork is killing me."

"It's okay," I told him comfortingly. "You're doing awesome. And look on the bright side. Next week will be an entirely different challenge, but at least it won't be footwork again."

"Bright side." He snorted, hit the button to turn off the music, and then looked over at me. "So what are you wearing tonight?"

I gave him a little frown. "Tonight? What's tonight?"

"The network's having a kickoff party. I was told all the regulars were invited and the celebrities. Didn't you get an invite?"

Embarrassment swept through me. I stepped backward, pulling out of his arms. "I guess not. I'm not really a regular, you know. I'm just a fill in for Svetlana." And what a way to remind me. Ouch. This one was going to leave a mark for a long, long time. I tried not to let it bother me, even though I couldn't help but get depressed.

A kickoff party for the show, and I hadn't even been invited. Man. That was cold. It did teach me something important, though—that I didn't count to the network.

"Aw, hell. I didn't know. I'm sorry, Zara. I thought everyone was invited."

I forced a bright smile to my face. "Hey, it's okay. Not your fault. I'll just stay here and practice."

"Hell, no." Ty set his jaw. "You're going to go as my date."

Well, if there was one thing I was learning about Ty, it was that he was loyal…and constantly full of surprises. "You want me to go as your date? Really?"

"Really."

I had a funny little flutter in my stomach. Anxiousness? Something else? "They're letting people bring dates to the party?"

He gave me a wicked look, and put his hand on my waist again, drawing me in for more dancing. "I'm not going to ask."

Oh no. That was not good. Being a party crasher wasn't smart if I wanted to be hired permanently by the network. "I'm not sure that's such a good idea, Ty."

"They want me on their show? They'll let me bring a date." His hand clasped mine firmly. "Now. Shall we try this again?"

A FEW HOURS LATER, WE WERE STILL A STEP BEHIND THE MUSIC, BUT making progress. We'd left practice early to prepare for the shindig, and I'd showered and toyed with my hair nervously for the past hour. I hadn't packed anything super fancy, but I did have a little black dress. Years of last-minute tweaking on costumes had made me handy with a needle and thread and last minute alterations. I managed to tear the back and sleeves off and changed it to a slip-dress with an open back and no sleeves. I had hair ribbons (what good ice skater didn't carry a batch of hair ribbons?) and used a few of those to add a splash of pink to my neck as a decorative choker. It wasn't super dressy, but it'd do. I had a pair of black sling-backs that I always packed and slipped those on, focusing my attention on my hair and makeup. If I did them well enough, no one would notice that my dress was a little on the casual side.

I fixed my hair into loose waves that spread over my shoulders and back. It was so dark brown that it was almost black, and it was layered so that it hung in sexy waves when I decided to let it out of my uptight bun. I lined my eyes and put on smoky eye shadow and mascara, and I curled my lashes to make my eyes bigger. Satisfied, I finished the look with a slick of nude lip gloss. The woman that stared back at me in the mirror was still tiny, but she had a hint of sultriness to her. My eyes—and naked back—looked sexy. At least no one would think I was fourteen tonight.

Ready, I left my room and headed into the living room of the cottage where Ty was waiting for me. I was surprised to see him in a gray suit—and a little dismayed. "How formal is this party?"

"Does it matter? It's too late to change anyhow." He gave me an up and down look, as if appraising my outfit.

I gave a small twirl in my modified dress. "Will I pass muster?"

"Absolutely." Ty rubbed his mouth, studying me, and then shook his head.

"What?"

"Was just wondering how come this girl doesn't show up to rehearsals every day. She's fucking hot."

I batted him on the shoulder. "I'm the same girl, doofus."

"Yes, but this one has, like, hair and stuff." He touched it in wonder.

"You're one to talk," I said, reaching out and rubbing his shaved scalp. "And if you saw this hair at five in the morning, I'd like to see what you could do with it."

He gave one of my locks a tug, and then rubbed it between his fingers. "If I saw this hair at five in the morning, it'd be because it was spread all over my pillow."

I sucked in a breath at the mental image. Ty leaning over me, me under him, my hair spread in a halo on the pillow. Just like that, I felt my nipples stiffen. Okay, wow. *Thanks for the visual.* Now I was all turned on.

He winked at me, as if to nullify any flirty implications. "Come on, Zara. Time to go party." And he offered me his arm.

I took it, smoothing my hand over his jacket sleeve. He looked hot tonight, too. The jacket hung just loosely enough to emphasize his big, meaty shoulders, but it cut in to hug his trim waist. He didn't wear a tie—no surprise there, because I doubted his thick neck would squeeze into one. Instead, his collar was open at the throat, showing darkly tanned skin against the pale blue of his shirt. He was freshly shaven and smelled fantastic.

I sniffed him. "Wow. Why doesn't this great-smelling guy show up to practice?"

"Oh, he can if you want him to." And Ty winked at me again.

I snorted. "Let's just go already. I'm freaked enough as it is."

"Don't be nervous," he told me, and his expression was grim, firm. "You have every right to be there, just as much as anyone else."

And that kind of made me feel warm inside. If nothing else, I had the support of Ty the MMA Biter.

Chapter Six

So... Okay, so that comment I made about Zara being hot? It was true, but I also didn't mention that I find her hot all the time. Like 24/7. Even in her leotards. There's just something about a girl that can pull her ankle over her head. —Ty Randall, Preliminary Practice Rounds, Ice Dancing with the Stars

THE PARTY WAS AN INTIMIDATING AFFAIR. THERE WERE SUITS EVERY-where, clearly network aficionados. A few of the stars from last season had shown up, along with the heavily pregnant Svetlana, Ty's manager, Chuck, and a few other VIPs.

I wasn't good at working a crowd, so I stuck to Ty's side like glue. He turned out to be incredibly charming, much to my surprise. Everyone knew his name and had a friendly word for him. Annamarie Evans had flirted heavily with him, giving me meaningful looks that indicated that she thought I should leave. I even tried to, but Ty's arm remained tight around my waist.

The female executive from that first meeting had showed up, too.

"Gloria," Ty said, holding his hand out for her to shake. "You look lovely tonight. You remember Zara, my partner?"

I held my hand out. "Hi again," I said awkwardly.

"How are things going?" Gloria asked politely, her gaze moving back to Ty. "Ready for the premiere tomorrow?"

"As ready as we'll ever be," Ty said, looking over at me. "Right?"

"Absolutely," I said, and began to gush nervous words. "Ty's footwork is just a bit of a step behind during the main chorus sequence, but I'm sure that we'll have it down by tomorrow once we get our costumes. I mean, we can take the day to practice and make sure we nail it in time. All it takes—"

Ty gave my waist a bit of a squeeze, cutting me off. "We'll be ready," he told her. "Don't you worry."

She gave us a patient smile. "I'm sure you will be. Enjoy the party, will you?"

"We will," Ty said. "Next time, though, do me a favor and make sure that Zara's invite gets to her? I think it got lost, and I'd hate for one of the assistants to get fired over something so small."

One eyebrow rose. She looked at me, and then gave Ty a curt nod. "I'll speak with the staff."

"See that you do," Ty said, and walked away, dragging me along with him.

My eyes felt like they were the size of saucers as we left her behind and stepped down onto a lovely garden terrace. "You just told her to invite me to the next one."

"I did. They have these fairly regularly. It's a good networking opportunity. You should go to all of them."

I didn't tell him that I probably wouldn't have the chance to go to another. I was just the fill in for Svetlana, after all. "I'll keep that in mind."

He gave me a long look. "Maybe don't talk too much, though."

I grimaced. "Yeah, I'm a nervous talker."

"You're a talker, full stop," he said, but he gave me another comfortable squeeze at my waist, his thumb grazing my bare back by accident.

A waiter passed by with glasses of champagne, and I snagged one. God, I needed a drink. I was nervous as hell.

Ty just as quickly took it back out of my hand again, and set it down on a nearby table. "You haven't exactly shown me that you can hold your alcohol," he murmured into my ear.

I started to get annoyed...and then realized he had a point. Drinking was probably bad the night before a performance, too. "You're right. It might mess up my juju."

He laughed, shaking his head at me. "Heaven forbid we mess up the juju."

"You laugh, but the juju's important," I chastised him.

"I'm sure it is," he said, giving me a warm look. His thumb stroked the small of my back again, and I was pretty sure that time it wasn't an accident. "I'm thinking a lot of things are important that I didn't notice before."

"Oh? Like what?" I tilted my head, regarding him. A curl of my hair slid over my shoulder, and I noticed Ty's gaze follow it.

An electric current ran through my skin, tingling with awareness.

"Ty! Ty, honey, come over here!" A female voice cooed, interrupting our intimate conversation. I looked over, and Annamarie was waving at Ty, trying to beckon him over to a group of her friends. All dressed in long, slinky gowns, all clearly models. Ugh.

And here I was, skinny Zara Pritchard, thinking I was having a moment with sexy, brawny Ty Randall. I was clearly dreaming.

I stepped out of his protective embrace and gestured. "You should go see what they want."

He glanced at them, and then at me. "I'll be right back."

"I'll be here," I said with a twirl of my finger. I crossed my arms over my chest and sat down on a stool at the nearby bar, waiting. I tried not to focus too much on how lovely Annamarie's group was, but it was impossible not to notice. She and her friends immediately pulled Ty in to their group, and the conversation flew at a lively pace. Annamarie would throw her head back and laugh and lean a little closer to Ty, nudging him with her arm.

Ugh. Wasn't she supposed to be sleeping with her own partner already? Why go after mine? I crossed my legs, and my foot swung over and over again in a nervous flick.

"Hello again," said a voice, and a big body slid into the stool next to mine.

I looked over in surprise. Serge. Speaking of Annamarie's partner... "Hi Serge. Long time no see."

"It *has* been quite a long time. Two weeks, perhaps?" He gave me a smile that was supposed to be sexy, I guessed, but his shaggy, too-long blond hair screamed 70s Eurotrash—as did his beaky nose—and it was hard to take him seriously.

"I meant in competition. What's it been, since 2002 Nationals?"

He gave me a pitying smile. "Oh, little Zara. This isn't a real competition. You realize this, yes? This is just a TV show we do for cash and notoriety. It is like an endorsement deal. You sell yourself for money, and try not to feel dirty about it afterward." He gave me a superior look down his long eagle-nose. "But I guess you would not know about that, would you?"

Oh, so that was what this conversation was about. Time to psych out the competition? Fine then. "No, I guess I wouldn't." I gave him a polite smile. "So how are those hemorrhoid ads working out for you?"

Serge actually advertised a muscle cream over in Europe, but as jokes went, it was close enough to offend. He glared at me. "I do not advertise for hemorrhoids."

"No? I thought I heard that. Oh, that's right." I snapped my fingers. "I heard that you were working hard on getting the herpes market cornered. My bad." I leaned in. "I'd tell you that you might wanna warn Annamarie about that, but it looks like she's currently sinking her hooks into my partner. Sorry."

He got up from his seat. "You are still an unpleasant little girl, I see. I came over to give you some friendly advice, and you have been nothing but rude."

I kept my smile pinned to my face. "Friendly advice, huh? What about?"

Serge gave me a thin-lipped smile. "Half the points come from scoring, little one. Half comes from the audience. If you want to win this? You need them both. But I see you don't care about winning."

I digested this warning-slash-advice. He couldn't influence the audience, of course, so he had to be warning me about the judging panel. So they were crooked? Great. Figure skating had a long history of 'slanted' judging panels, so this shouldn't have been a surprise to me, but I did feel a twinge of doubt.

I glanced over at my partner as Serge stalked away. Ty was laughing it up with Annamarie and her supermodel buddies, and I noticed Annamarie had a long, too-tan hand on his back, an almost possessive gesture. And he sure wasn't fighting her off.

Figured.

"No," Ty said. "Absolutely fucking not."

I bit my lip, glancing around nervously at the stage hands rushing around. People were everywhere, even crawling around in the dressing rooms, and so were the cameramen. No place was off limits, and that included last minute costume, ahem, alterations.

Ty threw down his shirt and looked at me with disgust. "What did I tell her all week?"

"No sequins," I said, biting the inside of my cheek and trying not to laugh.

"And what is this freaking…monstrosity covered with?" He gestured at the garish shirt that was now wadded into a ball.

I picked it up and studied it. It was a virtual match to my own, which meant it was incredibly hideous. It was a cowboy outfit…sort of. To go with our "Boot Scootin'" theme. Sort of. Except it was neon. I was neon pink and he was chartreuse. And both were covered in yellow fringe going up the arms (which was bad enough) and purple sequins (which was even worse). To make matters worse, I had bright white chaps and he had purple ones. Again, sequined and covered in fringe. His cowboy hat was bright green, and we had fake 'boots' that went over our skates and matched our chaps.

It was pretty much a costuming nightmare. No wonder they hadn't wanted to show us until the last minute.

Ty shook his head at me. "I'll wear the goddamn ugly hat. I'll wear the fucking fringey-ass pants, since I have to, but I refuse to wear sequins. Absolutely and completely refuse. NO fucking way."

I studied his clothing. It really was an odd choice for a guy as masculine as Ty. Maybe for a traditional figure skater with no sense of taste? But not Ty Randall, big, beefy, incredibly sexy MMA fighter. They didn't even show off his tight ass.

I shook my head at myself. Where on earth had those thoughts come from?

"I'm sorry, Zara," Ty said to me. He took my hands in his and gave me an earnest look. "I tried really fucking hard these last two weeks. I did. I understand how badly you want this. But a man's got to draw a line somewhere, and this is my line. If they have to scratch us from the competition, I'll take the scratch and work on another way to fix my PR."

"It's not that bad," I told him, giving his hands a squeeze.

"I look like I belong in a gay pride parade."

Okay, he kind of did. I studied his costume and then sighed. We could either spend the next hour warming up for the show, or I could try to fix his costume. Looking into Ty's angry gaze, it was clear what my choice was. I pulled up one of the folding chairs and got out my costume alteration kit. "Let me see what I can do."

Forty-five minutes later, Ty no longer looked like a parade float. We'd scrapped the shirt entirely, as well as the hat, and he'd decided to go bare-chested at my suggestion. After all, he had a gorgeous chest. Seemed a shame not to put that to good use. I couldn't do anything about his sequined boot-covers, so we ditched them. Instead, I focused on de-fringe-ing his pants and removing the strips of sequins that had been badly sewn down the seam of each leg. When I was done, he had garish neon pants, but now they just looked like they matched mine.

"Do you want a hot pink bandanna?" I asked as he pulled on his pants again. "It could complete the outfit."

He scowled at me. "Do I *look* like I want a hot pink bandanna?"

I giggled. Guess not. "Does this mean we can still go on?"

"I guess so," he said, and sighed heavily. "The guys are going to give me such shit for this."

THE MUSIC WENT UP, AND THE SHOW BEGAN. I COULD HEAR THE audience cheering from the Crash Room—horribly named, I thought—in the back where teams sat and waited for their turn to go out on the ice. The judges were introduced, and then a montage of clips from the past two weeks began, showcasing moments from our introductions to trainings.

I could hear a swell of gasps come up from the audience and heard my own voice, loud and tinny, over the speakers, explaining how I'd tripped and fallen. Oh no. They were showing the video of my bruised and swollen face.

At my side, Ty clenched my hand and rubbed his chin, clearly nervous about how it would go over. But then they cut away to another team, and laughter filled the studio a moment later as Michael Michaels had a montage of clips of him falling on his ass repeatedly.

No big drama about my nose, then. Good. I relaxed, too, and touched the bridge of it. It had healed up nicely a week ago, and you couldn't even tell that it had ever grown to the size of a potato.

The makeup artists had taken their time with me before the show, making sure that I looked like the others…which meant lots of make-up in bright colors. I wasn't surprised. Skaters were used to heavy eye-makeup, blush, and lipstick so you didn't look featureless and washed out on the ice. Of course, I was also used to my hair being pulled into an ultra-tight bun so it wouldn't get in my face, and they'd insisted on braiding it into two cutesy tails over my ears. Ugh. It went with my horrible psychedelic cowgirl costume, I supposed.

I eyed the costumes of the other contestants. Most of them wore a more casual look—jeans and plaid for the guys, denim dresses for the girls, and some sort of cowboy hat or fringe motif. We were the only ones in garish colors, and judging from the sympathetic looks Emma was sending my way, we looked pitiful. Oh well.

We were the first up after the montage, and I tried not to be nervous. Well, tried and failed. I've always had a bit of nerves before a performance, and this was no different. Except the difference here was that in Nationals or at the Olympics, I'd be given time on the ice to warm up and prep. On the show, we were expected to take care of that beforehand and just stroll out onto the ice, ready to skate as soon as the music started.

I didn't like that, but no one asked me. So I simply leaned over and touched my talismans taped to the bottom of my skate with my free hand, trying to increase my good juju.

"Okay, first team, you're up. Montage ends in sixty seconds," one of the production team told us, then pressed a hand to the headset over his ear. He pointed to the door at the far end of the Crash Room. Another assistant opened it and beckoned for us to come through.

In a daze, I stood. Ty grabbed my hand again and pulled me forward, and the butterflies in my stomach turned into pterodactyls. I stumbled after him, my legs feeling wooden. We were about to be on TV. National TV. Live TV. And Ty still didn't have the routine down pat. How could he? He wasn't a skater, and we'd only had two weeks to learn it. I didn't blame him. It was the show. The entire set-up was stupid. *I* was stupid for even agreeing to be on it. He'd look terrible and then, thanks to our ugly costumes, we'd be the laughing-stock of the figure skating world. And, oh God—

"Breathe, Zara," Ty told me as we moved into place. A cameraman was there in our faces, filming us as we waited, and I could hear the host talking to the audience, explaining the rules. There was a bit of chatter from the judges' panel, and then more from the host. The audience began to clap again, and my panic grew once more.

"Okay, in thirty seconds, you guys are going to step right out onto the ice, wave to the audience, and then get into position," the assistant told us. "Take off your blade guards now so you can be ready." She held her hand out.

I did so, obediently—so did Ty. As we did, I looked at the big red curtain that would pull back in mere seconds, cuing us to step onto the ice. There was a problem. I looked at the assistant. "I need to kiss the ice first."

"What?" She shook her head, taking my skate guards and tucking them under her arm. "Music's starting. Get ready to go out."

"I can't go out onto the ice unless I kiss it first," I said, and my voice raised to a hysterical note that was quickly drowned by the clapping of the audience. "It's bad luck. I can't do that! It's bad enough that we're going first!"

"Zara," Ty said calmly, "It's okay."

"It's not okay," I babbled, turning towards him with a panicked look. I tried to move forward to the curtains. I didn't care how stupid it'd look; if they'd let me just stick my head out and kiss the ice really fast, I'd be fine. My nerves would disappear because I'd have luck on my side. It didn't matter how torn up or dirty the ice was—I always kissed it. *Always.* "I have to do this, Ty. I have to. I can't—"

"Listen, Zara," Ty said, grabbing my hands before I charged through the curtains in my panic. "Listen," he said soothingly. "They're not going to let you kiss the ice—"

"First, no warm up, and now I can't kiss the ice?" I asked hysterically. Tears were pooling in my eyes. I was going to hyperventilate. I couldn't breathe. "I can't—"

"I know," he said, and his voice was calm. He squeezed my hands. "It's okay. I understand. Do you know what I do when I'm about to go out into a fight? For good luck?"

"Time to go out," the assistant said, urgency in her voice.

We ignored her. My gaze was locked on Ty's face. I needed reassurance, and I needed it badly.

He let go of my hands. "My coach and I have a secret handshake," he told me in a calm voice. He grabbed my hand, made a fist, fist-bumped me, and then grabbed my fingers and made a loop. Then he looped his own through it. He did three or four more hand motions before he was satisfied. "There. Lucky handshake. It'll counteract the bad juju, okay?"

"Okay," I whispered.

"Go out," the assistant hissed, giving us a little shove. "We're live, damn it!"

Ty winked at me, grabbed my hand, and then surged forward through the curtains. I had no choice but to follow.

After being backstage in the dark prep-room behind the curtains, gliding out onto the brightly-lit ice was blinding. The audience rose up into a wild cheer, and both Ty and I raised our free hands to wave at the crowd, moving to the center of the ice, our hands locked.

Ty stopped, digging his toe-pick into the ice, and then he pulled me close. We got into our starting pose, froze in place, and waited. As I stared at him, my hand clasped in his, I realized his palms were sweating, and he was more nervous than he'd let on. Strangely enough, now that we were on the ice, all my nerves had gone away.

So, I winked at him to let him know everything would be okay.

The music began, assaulting us with the thick guitar twang of "Boot Scootin' Boogie." We jumped into the dance, our hands tightly clasped, and began to perform to the music. I wore my brightest smile, trying to make this seem like fun, since the look on Ty's face was one of pure concentration. He was supposed to smile at me and look at ease; we'd practiced that multiple times. But it seemed he couldn't smile and do footwork at the same time, so I settled for footwork.

The chorus swelled, and we began the first footwork sequence, our skates moving fast and in-sync on the ice. Perfect! I knew we'd nailed it when I'd heard the audience clapping, and we continued on through the song.

Somewhere in the second half, Ty began to slow down. Perhaps it was too much to concentrate on, or maybe his nerves were getting to him, but I tried to cover for it as best as possible, making my moves a little more sweeping to disguise the fact that he wasn't quite able to keep up with the song. By the time the chorus moved through a second time, though, we were a full step behind. Nothing to do but carry on and persevere.

We only had a minute and a half to perform, so the song was truncated. I wanted to wince when the music ended before our dancing did. We flung our hands out into our finale pose, ignoring the fact that we were a step or two off, and the audience burst into applause.

We'd survived the first skate. I sucked in a breath and looked over at

Ty, grinning.

He yanked me forward and pulled me into a hug, plastering my smaller form against his big, naked chest. The audience cheered even more, and we hugged even more, and then we gave another wave to the crowd as the host skated over.

Maybe I hadn't been paying attention to the show itself, but the host I recognized. Chip Brubaker, who hosted a ton of these types of shows, moved over to us, a little wobbly on his skates. He wore a tux, a pound of makeup, and a fake smile. "Ty and Zara," he announced. "Our first skate of the evening. Give it up for them!"

We smiled and waved as the audience cheered again.

"Let's give our judges a minute to tally their scores," Chip said, and moved closer to us. "Ty, I notice you're missing half of your costume."

The host shoved a microphone towards Ty for him to answer.

After a moment's hesitation, Ty leaned in and spoke. "I am."

Chip took the microphone back, all goofy smiles. "Any particular reason for that?" Again, the microphone went right under Ty's nose.

"Sequins," Ty said immediately. "I'd rather be naked than wear sequins."

The audience gave a startled laugh, and I could hear whistles from one section.

Chip chuckled, as if pleased with our answer. "All right then." He turned to the cameras. "For those at home, just a reminder of how the scoring works. Fifty percent of the ice dancers' score will be based on our judges' criteria. They'll be looking for artistic performance, originality, and technical expertise, and they'll be scaling our dancers on a score of one to ten. The other fifty percent of the scoring will be based on your vote. If you like a couple and want to save them, vote. The phone number for voting for Zara and Ty will be on your screen." He pointed at the air, and I guessed that was where the phone number would show up. "Your favorites need your vote. And with that, let's go to our judges' panel and see how Zara and Ty did!"

We turned, and the spotlight went to the first person in the judges' panel. Penelope Marks, my old nemesis. When I'd walked off the ice at the Olympics? She'd gone on to medal despite having a totally inferior program. I hated her. She also got two of the endorsement deals that had been courting me until that moment. To say that I wasn't a fan was putting it mildly.

She looked gorgeous, if a little too tanned. Her limp blonde hair was cut in a jagged style, and she dripped with designer jewelry. She waved to the audience when they cheered, and then gave us a bright, pastel-pink smile, clasping her hands together. "So, Ty and Zara. First of all, I want to say that I appreciate how hard it is to come out here and perform." She gave us a polite smile. "I know it's tough, and ice skating is not for everyone. That being said, I do think you both need to work on your form and your footwork along with your artistry. I just wasn't feeling it at all." She held up a scorecard. "Sorry."

She'd given us a two.

Bitch.

The audience gasped. A few courteous 'boos' echoed.

Penelope shrugged. "I just didn't love it. Better luck next week."

The spotlight moved to the next judge, Irina Brezhlova. She was a Czech coach from back in the day, and very famous. Her motherly smile beamed down on us. "I thought you both did very well for being the first team to come out onto the ice. I wasn't a fan of the music, but I enjoyed your colorful costumes and the fun routine." She held up her card. Six. Getting better, at least.

The audience clapped politely.

The third judge was Raul Pacheco, a male skater that I vaguely recognized from the decade before mine. He studied us for a minute. "Your timing was off, but I think you both have potential. I'd like to see what you bring to future performances."

He unveiled another six.

"All right. That's a total of fourteen points out of a possible thirty." Chip patted me on the back since I was closest to him. "We'll see how that stacks up against the rest of our contestants. Thank you again, Ty and Zara."

We waved to the audience and then skated away, heading back to the Crash Room.

We were hosed.

Bad juju had totally nailed us.

THE REST OF THE SHOW WENT BY IN A BLUR. THE OTHERS PERFORMED, but I barely noticed except that Michael Michaels completely fell on his ass at one point. They had come back to us for one more question, which Ty had glibly answered while I'd sat there, numb. My mind kept playing back the scores. Penelope Marks had given us a two. I seethed at that two. It was like she was deliberately trying to torpedo us. We hadn't been great, but we hadn't been that bad. The score had been totally unfair.

Most of all, it bothered me that she'd openly screw Ty just because she didn't like me. That wasn't fair to him.

At the end of the show, all the scores were tallied and teams were sent back out onto the ice in the order of our scores. At the front of the lineup, Serge and Annamarie were tied with Toby and Victoria Kiss. Next was Jon Jon and Julia, then Emma and Louie Earl. Ty and I were tied with Tatiana and Michael Michaels for last.

The music went down, and the show was over.

Chapter Seven

So that competition thing? That was a total hoser. What was the point of me coming on this show again? To prance around with a sexy partner and then wash out in the first round? What the hell? Huh? Sexy partner? Yeah, I said that. Have you seen Zara? That tight little ass? It takes everything I have not to try and grab it, because that'd make me a perv. — Ty Randall, Post-Show Interview, Week 1, Ice Dancing with the Stars

THAT NIGHT, WHEN WE RETURNED TO THE COTTAGE TOGETHER, I headed straight for Ty's fridge (that was now plugged in), searching for beer.

"What are you looking for?"

"A drink," I told him. "I think I need one after tonight."

He snorted. "I thought it went better than expected. The audience liked us."

"Yeah," I told him. "But the judges hated us, and that's half of our score."

"Come on," he told me, pulling me away from the fridge that was now filled with health foods and bottles of water—curse my interference! —and pulled me toward the sofa. "You didn't really expect to win, did you?"

I thumped down on one end of the couch and gave him a look that said, "Yes, I did expect to win."

He laughed, sitting on the other end of the couch, and grabbed my feet, pulling off my tennies to make me comfortable. I let him put my feet in his lap. A foot massage was obviously meant to distract me...but I was game for a bit of distraction. I crossed my arms over my chest and wiggled my feet as he tossed my shoes to the ground and began to rub them through my socks.

"That first chick that was the judge," he said. "What was her name?"

"Penelope Marks," I said sourly. "A really old enemy of mine."

"I think she hates everyone. Did you see that she gave Michael Michaels and his chick a one? She's clearly supposed to be the mean judge." He rubbed my foot and then frowned at my red-and-yellow-striped socks. "Didn't you wear these yesterday?"

"I wear them every day during competition," I said, wiggling my toes at him.

"Gross?" He released my feet.

I laughed and poked him in the stomach with my big toe. "I wash them in the sink every night, silly."

He put his big hands back on my feet, and that smile that made my stomach tie into knots tugged at his mouth. "Let me guess. More juju?"

I nodded, and then sighed. "Not that it mattered. Between the lack of an ice kiss and Penelope on the judging panel, I'm pretty sure we're screwed."

"You worry too much," he told me easily. "It's fine."

"And you're not worrying at all," I complained at him. "Don't you care if we get totally reamed by the judges? The longer you stay on the show, the better you'll do, PR-wise."

"Yeah, but if it means ripping sequins out of my clothing every night five minutes before we're supposed to go on stage? I'll take my chances." Silence fell between us, and Ty looked over at me. "Did you see the others' costumes?"

"No," I said sulkily. "I was too busy being blinded by ours."

He chuckled. "Yeah. Imelda has some shit taste in costumes."

"And routines, and music."

"I kinda think we're hosed either way," he told me.

That just made me feel worse. Tears brimmed in my eyes. "I hate losing."

"Oh, come on," he told me, and he grabbed my calves, dragging me forward. He pulled me until my legs dangled over his lap and my butt rested against one of his big thighs. "Don't cry. Do you need a hug?"

He spread his arms and gave me a silly puppy-dog look that made me laugh despite my tears. "You're really taking this 'kinder, gentler Ty Randall' thing to heart, aren't you?" I teased, leaning in and putting my head on his shoulder.

Ty hugged me close, rubbing my back. "I know it sucks to work this hard on something and get nowhere. We just have to do the best we can. That's all we can do. Fuck the rest of them."

I wiggled closer, enjoying being cuddled against Ty. He was so big and strong and...cuddly. You wouldn't think that a tough guy bulging with muscle could be cuddly, but he was warm and comfy to lean against, and I liked the way his big hands rubbed my shoulders and back. I snuggled closer, sighing. "I feel like I failed you. Like I failed us. Just because Penelope Marks hates me."

"You didn't," he whispered. His hand stroking my back slowed, and I felt his fingers trail slowly up and down my spine. "You did awesome. It's her fault if she can't see that."

We said nothing for a long moment. His hand continued to move slowly up and down my spine, sending little shockwaves through my nerve endings. To my embarrassment, I felt my nipples harden. Awareness moved through me, and I felt heat pooling between my legs, my pulse pounding as he continued to lightly brush his fingertips over my back, and I could feel him through the thin material of my t-shirt. I didn't move, I simply breathed in the scent of Ty from where my head was nestled against his neck. His big neck. Odd that I liked a guy with such a thick neck. I'd thought it was a sure sign of a dumb jock at first, but Ty was clever, and determined, and I really liked him the more I hung out with him.

Which was totally bad news.

I pulled away with a small, reluctant sigh, not trusting that I wouldn't somehow embarrass myself around him.

"Thanks for the comforting," I told him, trying to keep my voice chipper and hide the fact that I wanted to crawl all over him and put my mouth on his. I wasn't his type—a stick with a mouth, he'd called me. Annamarie Evans was his type, and I was nothing like her. "I think I'll head to bed. I'm going to be useless until they give us the results tomorrow anyhow."

He nodded and cleared his throat. "Sounds good. You going to practice early?"

Part of me wanted to pout and hang up my skates for good, but I'd learned my lesson about that. "Yeah. I'll be up at dawn as usual. I figure if we move on, we have to have a new routine learned by next week's show. We'll need all the help we can get."

Ty chuckled. "Good point. I'll be there, too."

I gave him a faint smile. "Night."

"Night."

WAITING FOR THE LIVE SHOW'S RESULTS, THE NEXT DAY PASSED SLOWLY. We only had a half day of training, since the rest had to be spent getting ready for being on-air that evening. Imelda hadn't shown up, but she had sent over an assistant with notes for us. Next week's theme would be 'theatrical soundtracks,' and she'd picked a theme from *The Maltese Falcon* that I didn't recognize. She'd left a note that she was already working with costuming on our outfits, so not to worry about it.

The element added this week? The pair spin.

We skipped practicing that for now, since it wouldn't matter if we had to learn it or not if we were voted out. Ty and I took it easy, going through the steps of the new and equally-boring routine that Imelda had picked out for us.

I was starting to wonder if our choreographer was in cahoots with Penelope and if they were determined to make us the most boring team out there.

"WE HAVE THE RESULTS FROM LAST NIGHT'S VOTING," CHIP SAID. "MAY I have the envelope, please?" He paused for dramatic effect as a young child skated out to him with the big red envelope.

My hand clenched Ty's sweaty one.

So far, the results show hadn't been nearly as painful. It was only a half-hour long, which meant there was time for a montage recap of the prior night, some commentary from the judges, a singer to trot out and flog their latest single, and then the results. We'd all paraded around the ice one last time in our costumes from the night before, and then we'd lined up in the order of our scores.

"Before we read the results, I'd like to see who our judges think will go home?" He looked to the judging panel.

Oh no. My lip curled. This was going to be like salt in the wound, wasn't it?

Penelope played with a pen on the judging table, tapping it as she thought. "I considered this for a little while last night, and I feel like the weakest link is Ty and Zara. They should be the ones to go home."

I made a gagging face, and then remembered that we were on camera. I hoped they hadn't caught that. The way the audience laughed, though, they had clearly seen my expression. I'd have to remember that for next time.

"And you, Irina? Who do you think should go home?"

"I feel," she said in her thick accent, "that all of the teams did well. I don't think I could choose someone to go home at this point. They've all worked really hard."

Clearly Irina was the softball judge. The audience clapped, agreeing with her.

"And Raul?"

He considered for a moment. "I thought Jon Jon and Julia had no chemistry. My vote would be for them."

That surprised me. I glanced down the line at Jon Jon, but judging from the look on his face, he'd been expecting something like that.

"Time for the results," Chip said. "Based on the audience votes and combined with the scores from last night…the first team safe is…Emma and Louie Earl!"

Triumphant music broke out, and I clapped for Emma, glad for her. She hugged her partner and looked thrilled as they skated forward, waved to the audience, and then moved off of the ice.

"The next team safe," Chip continued, waiting for the clapping to die down. "Is…Serge and Annamarie Evans!"

I clapped, though less enthusiastically for them. Neither one was a surprise there. Louie Earl was an older man who was surprisingly agile on his feet, and Emma was talented. Serge and Annamarie were both graceful and good-looking. They'd never be the first to go.

"The next safe…Toby and Victoria Kiss!" More clapping. That meant we were one couple away from being in the bottom two.

"The last couple safe is…Jon Jon and Julia Mckillip!"

Yep. Bottom two. I wrinkled my nose and looked over at Ty with an

I-told-you-so expression. Next to us were Michael Michaels and Tatiana. Tati looked pissed as hell, though she was smiling with gritted teeth. Poor Tati. Evidently she wasn't happy with the results. I didn't blame her. I knew Tati was a perfectionist, so her partner falling down mid-routine had to be bothering the crap out of her.

The spotlight focused on Ty and I, and another on Tati and Michael Michaels. My stomach churned nervously, and my hand clasped in Ty's was trembling.

"The team going home tonight…is…" Chip paused for dramatic effect.

I dug my toe-pick into the ice, ready to skate forward. I took a deep breath and sighed, closing my eyes. Goodbye, second chance.

"I guess the audience isn't a fan of sequins, either! Tatiana and Michael Michaels, you will be going home. Ty and Zara, you are safe for one more week!"

The orchestra began to play, and I opened my eyes, looking at Ty in shock. We were safe? Ty the MMA Biter had been saved by the audience vote? Holy crap.

He grabbed me around the waist and swung me around, grinning, and I clung to him. Holy crap. Holy crap, we were safe!

The audience clapped, and Ty and I were shuffled off the ice so Tati and her partner could do a last lap around the ice while the credits rolled and Chip yammered into his microphone.

We were safe one more week, despite everything. Maybe we stood a chance after all.

THE NEXT MORNING, I STUDIED THE BORING ROUTINE PAPER AND frowned at Imelda. "There's only one lift in this entire thing."

She sniffed and texted something into her phone, seated in a folding chair away from the ice, as usual. "This week's required element is the sit spin. Lifts aren't until next week."

"I know. But lifts are flashy and the audience always loves them." I skated toward her, a little frustrated. "Ty's a big strong guy. We can do more than one lift." I looked over at Ty. "Don't you think?"

He shrugged. "I can bench press two hundred. What do lifts involve?"

"We can always do an Ina Bauer for you, and I can do a handstand, or we could do a crouch and horizontal, or…" I stopped at the glazed look in his eyes. "Just trust me. You can pick me up, right?"

He snorted. "Duh. You weigh nothing."

"I'm not sure this is such a good idea," Imelda said in a prissy voice. "We need to keep things easy."

"This *will* be easy," I told her. I skated to Ty's side, and then turned my back to him, standing in front of him. "Can you lift me up?"

"How high?"

"Put your hands on my waist and pick me up as high as you can go."

Big hands grasped me at the hips, and he hefted me into the air as if I weighed nothing. I held my breath as he held me up to shoulder height. "You want higher?"

"That's good," I told him, keeping my body as straight as possible. "We could do something like this, or I can do the splits." I extended my legs outward as an example. "Or if he can hold me on the thighs, I can pull one leg over my head."

"So you *can* put a leg over your head?" Ty asked. "I thought you were joking when you told me that. Damn, girl. I think I want to see it for myself."

I blushed, dropping my legs, and patted him on the hand. "Put me down now."

He did, lightly, and I hopped away on the ice, hoping to hide my flustered sensibilities. "See?" I told Imelda. "We can work a few more lifts in there, and if we increase the difficulty, we should score better."

"I don't think so," she said again, and turned back to her phone.

I wouldn't be deterred. "We need more flash in this routine," I told her. "You basically just have us circling around on the ice for a minute and a half with two lifts. No one's going to be interested in that, especially not if we're dancing to the Maltese Falcon."

She ignored me.

"What about the costumes?" Ty asked, skating to my side and skidding to a stop (rather artfully, I noticed).

"Just a pinstriped suit for you and a white dress for her."

"Sequins?" Ty asked.

"Not many," Imelda said quickly.

He gave me a pained look.

Ugh. It was like she was ignoring everything we wanted to do. "You do realize we almost went home last night? This," I shook the printed out routine at her, "is going to ensure that we go home. It's boring!"

"I'm trying to keep in mind his capabilities and give the audience something appealing," Imelda said easily, and then she went back to her chair.

I wadded up the paper in disgust. She wouldn't come onto the ice with us. She had zero enthusiasm for her job. She made decisions without consulting us, and they were bad ones. "You know what? You're fired."

Her head popped up at that. "You can't fire me."

"Sure I can." I pointed at the door. "You're fired. Get out."

"The network appointed me," she said with a frown. "You don't get to decide."

The cameraman zoomed in on my face. I didn't care that they were filming. She was doing nothing but dragging us down. "The Maltese Falcon is boring. You didn't ask us if we wanted to dance to that, you just picked it. You're ignoring our requests for the routine. You're putting sequins on the costumes even though we've asked you not to—repeatedly. At this point, if we follow your routine, we're going home. At least if we do our own routine, we'll stand a chance. So if the network doesn't kick us out, we might have a shot in hell of staying. Like I said. You're fired."

Imelda huffed. "There're two of you on this team. I'm staying."

Ty skated to my side. "I agree with my partner. I think you need to go."

I gave Imelda a blissful smile. "Problem solved."

She stared at both of us, and then pointed her phone in my direction. "I'm calling the network."

"Call," I bluffed, skating away. "Either you walk out, or we do. Let's see which one they put on the show next week." And I skated away, just because I could. It wasn't like she'd follow me onto the ice, anyhow.

By the time I turned around again, she was gone, and Ty was there on the ice, arms crossed, giving me an impressed look.

I skated a circle around him, thinking. "You mad?"

He laughed. "Hell no. I was just thinking you have balls of steel sometimes."

I gave him a flirty look. "Don't fuck with me when I'm on the ice. That's my home territory."

"No kidding," he drawled, his look appraising. "I like it. So...what now?"

I thought for a moment, skating in circles around him. "This is different than regular figure skating competitions. We're pretty much fucked with the judging panel no matter what we do." Okay, so maybe that wasn't that different than some skating competitions. "We need the audience on our side. Which means we have to impress them. Dazzle them."

"Oh god. Dazzle. With sequins?"

I gave him a look. "Give me more credit than that?"

He chuckled. "Fine, fine. So tell me what you're thinking."

I continued to skate circles, thinking, my hands clasped behind my back. "We need to shock them somehow. This week's theme is cinematic. Movie stuff. We just need to find the perfect movie that fits in with who we are...." An idea dawned on me, and I snapped my fingers. Oh my god, it was perfect.

It was perfect *if* Ty went for it.

I skated toward him and put my hands on his shoulders, looking up at him. "Do you trust me?"

"As much as I can trust anyone in this chickenshit outfit," he said with a grin. "And as long as you don't dress me as one of the Village People, I'm fine."

"Nope," I said enthusiastically, heading to the edge of the ice and stepping off. I went to my workout bag and pulled out my phone, then searched the internet for a clip. When I found it, I went back to Ty and handed my phone to him, looking for approval.

He snorted at what I picked, even as the music began to stream out from my phone, tinny and muffled. "*Jaws*? Cute."

"That's right," I told him. "It *is* cute. People will think we're poking fun at ourselves. They won't expect it, and it'll catch their attention. It'll make you look like you have a sense of humor about the biting thing, and people will talk about it. That's exactly what we want. It defuses an ugly situation and shows we can laugh at ourselves while having fun."

He considered, staring at my phone for so long that I thought he was getting angry. Maybe I'd pushed too far and he'd tell me to fuck off. Maybe Ty didn't *have* a sense of humor about the whole biting thing. When I'd asked him before, he'd shrugged me off.

But as I watched, a slow smile spread across his face. He looked over at me, and chuckled again. "Balls of steel, all right."

Relief cut through me sharply, and I laughed. He wasn't mad at me. Thank goodness. "I figure we can shock them into loving us, or go home anyhow."

Ty regarded me. "So how do we skate to that music?"

I thought for a minute, and then grinned, my mind full of ideas. "We follow the pattern of the song. We can do slow movements at the start, and build up to the crescendo. When the crescendo hits, we can do a lift. You can put me on your shoulders, and I can raise a leg into the air. Oooh!" I clapped my hands. "I know. We can design a costume for me so that when I raise my leg into the air, it looks like a shark fin rising from the water."

He chuckled, shaking his head. "I'll admit, that's kind of cool. So what do I wear?"

"You can dress as the main guy from *Jaws*. In the black shirt and jeans. Glasses, the works. What was his name?" I snapped my fingers, trying to think.

"Brody."

"That's it. Something simple and masculine." I gave him an impish smile. "No sequins."

"I could kiss you for that right now."

I blushed. Hard. "No kissing necessary."

He chuckled. "Spoilsport. So…partner lifts. How do we work those in?"

I considered for a moment, and then held my hands out in our dancing position. "Let's try a few different things."

We experimented for a few hours and came up with a loose routine. I made notes and decided to work on the choreography in my spare time. Meanwhile, we set one of the production assistants on getting the music rights to *Jaws* and some concepts for costumes.

At least if we went down this time, we'd go down on our own terms.

Chapter Eight

Jaws, of all things. The girl's a genius, I have to admit.
—Ty Randall, Pre-Show Interview for Week Two

THE NEXT WEEK PASSED SURPRISINGLY QUICKLY, AND BEFORE I KNEW
it, it was competition night again. I was more nervous this time than
last time—Ty had our routine down pat, since a lot of it simply consisted
of hefting me into the air and gliding. Even our costumes were awesome,
right down to Ty's black mock turtleneck sweater and tight black pants.
He even had a big brown gun-belt, which was in the movie clips and was
a great touch that Ty himself had thought of. He wore a pair of wire-rim
glasses to complete the look.

My outfit was a plain, dark blue to about mid-calf, and then it changed
to gray. There were 'wings' tied to each leg that I was going to release about
halfway through our dance, and hopefully they would surprise everyone.

Ty and I had practiced day and night for this particular routine, and
I was so proud of it. We'd even worked with the production and lighting
crew to get the look just right.

This time, we'd drawn the last skate. Jon Jon and Julia Mckillip were
up first. I tried to pay attention to the other routines like Ty was, but I was
a bundle of nerves. I kept crossing my legs and reaching down to touch

my talismans over and over again, rubbing the newest—a sequin from last week's costume.

No one fell tonight. I couldn't watch the TV in the Crash Room—bad luck—but Ty had no such qualms. He'd lean in close every time a couple went on to ice skate, and he would give me a bit of a play by play.

"Jon Jon and Julia look pretty stiff," he'd tell me as the strains of 'Love Story' echoed in the room.

Then, "Emma's cute. They stuck to country again," he told me. "Nine to Five" played, and I could tell from the clapping of the audience that they were definitely into their theme. Good for Emma.

"Annamarie went for hotness, clearly," Ty told me with a chuckle when the next couple went on. I glanced at the TV, unable to help myself despite the bad juju, and rolled my eyes. The theme was clearly *Titanic*, but Annamarie had taken her own interpretation, her costume showing more skin than was probably legal in that time period, while Serge was dressed as Jack from the movie, complete with suspenders and rolled up white sleeves. I looked away again, quickly, when Annamarie ran her hands down her breasts in a showy motion.

"Damn," Ty said. "She's clearly here to win."

"Or to hook up," I muttered under my breath.

"Hmm?" Ty asked, leaning in to me.

"Nothing." I wouldn't look at the TV again if it killed me. No sense in psyching myself out.

Toby and Victoria were next. The familiar strains of "Hakuna Matata" from *The Lion King* filled the speakers. I heard Ty chuckle. "They look cute. They'll do well."

"You're not helping me," I told him, and I rubbed the talismans on the bottom of my skate even harder.

"You two are up," one of the production assistants called.

"Let's do this," Ty told me. He put an arm around my waist as we headed to the curtained staging area.

"Thirty seconds," the assistant whispered to us.

"You ready?" Ty murmured in my ear. It sent shivers through my body. He raised his fist, and I gave him a fist-bump back, and then we did the motions of his lucky handshake.

I smiled at him. "Juju is now in place."

"We are going to kick ass," he told me. Then he took my hand, and we skated out onto the center of the ice.

Our beginning 'pose' started with the two of us together. I stood in front of Ty, and his arms were wrapped around mine. As soon as the music began, we began to skate, the low notes soft and deceivingly smooth. No one was making a sound as we danced and skated our way around the ice, preparing for the first lift.

Then it began. The familiar, haunting chorus of Jaws with the ominous notes. As soon as it started, Ty raised me into the first lift, and I moved over him, my body flat, one of my legs raising into the air. The lights in the stadium had gone dim, and a spotlight shone on our lift.

The flaps in my pants were now undone, and when I raised my leg into the air, I did so slowly, even as Ty lifted me higher. With the gray of my costume and skate cover, and the surge of our movements, it mimicked the rising of a dorsal fin into the air.

There were ripples of shock and laughter in the audience, and then cheers.

The routine continued on. Ty gracefully let me down onto the ice and we clasped hands, moving to the music in a fluid motion that we'd practiced hard to make look so incredibly easy. Then, the crescendo rose again, and we did another "dorsal fin lift." This time, there were wild cheers from the audience.

I tilted my leg forward, and did a slow flip down Ty's front, landing on my skates as we began to dance once more. The hardest parts of the routine were done, and now we just needed to finish well. I'd added a spin for myself at the end, and Ty raised an arm over my head as I started to spin around like a top. I curved my leg in, whirling faster and faster as Ty continued to skate a wider circle around me. The swing of my specially-made pants flared outward; the dual colors making the spin more visually stunning than it really was.

The last few notes of our routine hit. I slammed to a stop and dropped into a dramatic dip. As we'd practiced, Ty was there to catch me inches before I smacked onto the ice, his hand behind my shoulders. We froze, waiting for the audience reaction.

There was a roar of applause.

Breathing hard, I grinned up at Ty, and we both got to our feet. I put my hand in his, and we waved at the audience. They were standing up. A giddy wave of excitement shot through me, and I gave Ty a triumphant look. See? We didn't suck after all.

Once the audience calmed down, Chip skated over to us.

Ty looped a casual arm around my shoulder, leaning in over my shoulder as I moved in next to the host.

"Well, that was original," Chip said with a laugh. "It's a big change from last week."

"We decided to take things into our own hands a bit more," I said with a smile, glancing over at Ty. "Show off our personalities."

"And *Jaws* does that?" Chip held the microphone out to us, waiting for a response.

Ty leaned in closer to me, his breath on my neck. "It's because I like to bite."

And he gave my ear a friendly, playful nip.

My eyes went wide, even as the crowd roared their appreciation. Catcalls filled the air. I hadn't expected his bite...or their reaction. Immediately, I blushed hard.

Thank god Chip didn't see my reaction. He turned away, facing the panel of judges. "Let's see what our panel thought of Ty and Zara's interpretation of *Jaws!*"

Penelope's mouth was thin, her arms crossed. She swiveled in her chair for a moment, and then picked up a score card. "Better than last week, but I'm still waiting to be wowed."

It was a four.

I exchanged glances with Ty. Figure skating was full of all kinds of bullshit scoring, but this was getting ridiculous.

"Well, I loved it," Irina said. "I thought it was playful and fun and very creative. We should see more routines like that."

And she gave us an eight.

"I agree," Raul said. "That was exciting and different. I'm impressed."

He also gave us an eight.

I squeezed Ty's hand excitedly. Our scores didn't suck this time. It didn't matter if we were in the middle of the pack as long as we weren't last and we didn't hose the popular vote.

We retreated backstage to the Crash Room. I sat down next to Ty on our bench and resisted the urge to rub my ear. It still tingled from his nip, and I was pretty sure my entire body was vibrating with intensity.

"That went well," I said breathlessly. "I think they liked it. The audience, that is. Not the judges. They never like us. Well, at least not Penelope. But the other two gave us good marks," I babbled.

He swiped at his face with a towel, and then nodded. "Yeah, it wasn't bad." He seemed so casual, as if it were every day that a guy just reached over and bit his partner's ear on national television.

"You surprised me," I blurted after a moment, unable to stand it any longer.

"Huh? Oh." Ty chuckled. "Yeah. I figured it'd be good to get the audience on our side as much as possible, and it seemed like a good idea at the time. Sorry if I freaked you out. I wasn't trying to scare you."

"You didn't...I wasn't—"

But now he was looking at me curiously. "You do know I'd never hurt you, right, Zara? That shit with me..." He rubbed his chin. "That was just heat of the moment in the cage. It's not really me."

I knew about that sort of thing. So I nodded. "No, I get it. Don't you worry about me."

Just for show. Nibbling on my ear, purely for show. Was I impressed with how clever my partner was? Or incredibly disappointed that it wasn't more personal?

THE NEXT NIGHT, WE WERE THE SECOND COUPLE MARKED AS SAFE.

"I knew it!" I said to Ty triumphantly as we skated off the ice and into the production area. An assistant was there, holding our blade guards, and we popped them on quickly. "We're here another week. That's awesome. I'm so excited!"

Ty grinned at me. He wasn't bubbling over with enthusiasm like I was, but he did seem pleased at our success. "We deserved it. You kicked ass."

"You weren't so bad yourself," I said loftily. We headed to the changing area, and Ty put his hand on the small of my back to guide me through the sea of people moving around us, still moving frantically since the show was still on. At least our part was done. "I think that ear thing was inspired."

"So was *Jaws*," he told me. "We should go out and celebrate, you know."

I felt a flutter of excitement at the thought. "Oh?"

"Yeah. Grab a bite to eat, get away from the whole gig for a few hours. Celebrate our awesomeness for a bit." He grinned at me, so boyish and gorgeous that I couldn't help but fall under his spell. "I think we could use some downtime."

"That sounds good." I glanced around the surging backstage area. "Should we invite the others?"

His brows drew together. "Why?"

So it didn't seem like a date? "Oh. Uh, no reason. I was just curious if you wanted to hang with Annamarie or something."

"Nah. Let's just go the two of us. It'll be easier to sneak out with a small party."

"Got it. Let me change." I headed into the girls' locker room, feeling a little weird. The flutter had taken up permanent residence in my stomach. Ty wanted to go out with just me? Even after we'd spent the last four weeks with solely each other? Really?

That was either…really flattering, or just more team building and that I was reading too much into.

I quickly showered, scrubbed my face off, and dressed. My hair was wet, so I pulled it into another tight bun and changed into my leotard and tights. I'd worn a sloppy plaid tee over the ensemble, and now I wished I'd worn something a bit…sexier. God, why did I suck so hard at being attractive?

I'd never really had a chance to date much. As in, at *all*. My teenage years had been spent on the ice, practicing, even after my flameout. I'd been homeschooled and was an only child, so I'd never been around a ton of guys. Later on, the kind of guys I met didn't understand my dedication to and drive for my ice-skating career, even though it had petered out long ago.

Plus, it was hard to meet men when you were dressed up as a pink dinosaur.

Basically, I had a lame dating track record. I could count the number of dates I'd had on one hand, and no one had ever gotten further than second base with me.

I was pretty sure Ty had a lot more experience than that.

This isn't a date, Zara, I reminded myself. We were skating partners, busy repairing our careers. I was reading a lot more into it than I should have been.

I swung my gear bag over my shoulder and ran into Emma as I left the locker room. "Hey," I told her. "Who got eliminated?"

"Jon Jon," she said with a grimace. "No surprise there, but he'll be really disappointed. But that partner of his just has no rhythm. Poor guy."

"That sucks," I said sympathetically. But someone had to go, and for tonight, I was glad it wasn't me.

She gave me a shrewd look. "That routine you did. That was pretty creative. I liked it."

I grinned at her. "Thanks. I figured if we didn't pull out some flash, we were going home tonight."

"You have Imelda, don't you? I had her last year." She grimaced. "And I requested not to have her again this year. Still, I'm surprised she came up with something so outrageous for you two."

"Had," I said flatly, hefting my bag. "I fired her. That routine was all me."

Her eyes widened. "Wow. I should ask you to help with my routine next week."

I stared at her awkwardly. If I helped her, it'd probably just assist me in getting voted off. "Uh, well…"

"I'm kidding." She laughed, and then gave me a wave. "See you on the ice."

"Bye." I escaped before we could have any other weirdly awkward conversations and met Ty outside of the locker room.

He grinned at me. "You ready to go?"

"Sure." I moved into step next to him. "So how are we going to do this? Do you have a car? Call a cab?"

"Nah." He put a hand to the small of my back again, guiding me out of the studio. "If I call a cab, that means a cameraman's going to follow us out, and I don't want the show tagging along. I called in a favor." He glanced around, and then gestured to an emergency exit. "Let's go out that way. Come on."

We slipped out a side door and headed out to alley behind the back lot of the studio. There was a black sedan waiting there, and as we approached, a driver got out.

So did Ty's manager, Chuck. He pointed at Ty with the cellphone that seemed permanently attached to his jaw most days. "You owe me."

"I do," Ty said easily. "Thanks for calling this in."

"If anyone at the network asks, you stopped for ice cream and took a wrong turn," he told the driver, peeling off a couple of twenties. "Understand?"

"Yes, sir," the driver said with a grin, and then glanced back at us. "Hop in."

Ty took my bag from my shoulder and tossed it in the trunk along with his. Then we got into the back seat.

The car pulled out of the parking lot and I glanced over at Ty. "So where are we going?"

"Well," he said, and patted his stomach. "I'm fuckin' starving, so I thought we'd get something to eat. That ok?"

"Fine with me." Like I was going to argue? I was heading out on a partner-not-a-date with Ty Randall, who was growing hotter and hotter with every day that passed. "What are we going to eat?"

"I know you're all health conscious and crap," he said. "What won't you eat?"

I wrinkled my nose, thinking. "Hot dogs?"

He laughed. "I can assure you we're not going to have hot dogs. Do you have a preference?"

"I guess not? Something healthy. We're working out hard in the morning again, and I don't want to mess up my system with something heavy and full of carbs."

He eyed me from across the seat. "You don't mind me saying, but you look like you could use a few carbs."

I stuck my tongue out at him. "That's right. I'm just a stick with a mouth, right?"

"And a pair of tits," he teased.

I shot him the bird.

"I'm kidding, I'm kidding. You look fine. If you were heavier, I probably wouldn't be able to lift you—"

This time, I knuckled him in the arm.

"Hey!" He laughed, mock-backing away from me. "I'm joking, I'm joking. How about sushi?"

"I like sushi," I agreed.

Chapter Nine

*Usually, the more I learn about a chick, the less I like her.
Strangely enough, Zara's the opposite. She's crazy, I mean, with
the health food and the juju-mojo shit she's constantly doing, but
there's a method to the insanity. And the more I find out about her?
The more I 'get' her. It's weird.* —Ty Randall, Practice Interview,
Ice Dancing with the Stars

WHEN WE GOT TO THE RESTAURANT, THERE WAS A LONG LINE OF people behind a cordoned rope, waiting to get in. I frowned at them through the car window. "Should we go somewhere else?"

"Nope. They know me here." He got out and opened the car door for me, and I slid out after a moment, feeling self-conscious in my grubby clothing and makeup-free face. All the people in line were dressed in trendy, flashy clothing, and they stared at us as we walked up. I noticed Ty put his hand at the small of my back again, leading me to the front of the line and bypassing the cordoned area.

He nodded at the maître d'.

"Mr. Randall," the man said, clearly excited. "Welcome back. Your regular table?"

"Anywhere you've got," he said easily and nudged me inside.

I raised my brows and looked over at Ty as we entered the swanky restaurant. "Regular table? You a big sushi fan?"

He laughed.

"What's so funny?" I crossed my arms over my chest, maneuvering through the sea of tight, white-tablecloth-covered tables. Each one was tiny, two chairs crammed close to it, and I had to watch myself to make sure I didn't bump anyone's elbows. The place looked pretty fancy.

"The last girl that asked me that wanted to ensure that I'd go down on her. Just sounded weird coming out of your mouth."

"What? No! That wasn't what I was—I mean—I didn't—"

"I know," he said with another chuckle. "Chill out."

We moved to the far side of the crowded restaurant to a private booth with deep, red seats and wooden accents. I slid in on one side, and Ty slid in next to me instead of going to the other. After my initial moment of surprise, I scooted over a bit more, trying not to blush.

Now this was *really* feeling like a date. Bad Zara, bad. No lusting after your partner. Hooking up while ice skating together? Everything I'd ever been told by other skaters said that it was some seriously bad juju.

And we had enough things working against our mojo at the moment.

A waiter set down two glasses of water and gave Ty an expectant look.

"Bottle of sake, please," Ty said. "Your best."

The waiter nodded and whisked away.

Ty glanced over at me. "You wanted to drink the other night. I figured this'd be your chance to get good and plastered."

"I've never had sake. Does it taste good?"

"That depends on your definition of good. It'll get you drunk, though."

"Fair enough," I told him, curiously excited about getting sloshed. Hey, first time for everything.

"So what's your story?" Ty asked me as the waiter returned with a tiny bottle and two even tinier shots. Ty immediately took the bottle and began to pour a teeny tiny shotglass for me, and then held it out.

"My story?" I took the tiny shot and sniffed it, not sure I liked the odor. It was cold, though. I'd wait for Ty to drink before trying it.

"Yeah. You don't drink, don't smoke, eat healthy food all the time, work out like a monster, and you're talented as hell. Yet you're on this show which, for all intents and purposes, is basically a regurgitation of a bunch of washed-up talent."

I blinked at that assessment. "I should remind you that you're on this show, too."

"I know," Ty told me, his voice blunt. He picked up his sake shot. "But I'll be the first one to tell you that I fucked up my career." He held his shot out to me.

I clinked mine to his. "To fuck-ups?"

"To fuck ups." He tipped his head back and downed the shot.

I sipped mine and immediately coughed. God, that was strong. At Ty's amused chuckle, I held my nose and downed the rest of the shot. It burned cold and oddly dry going down my throat, and I swallowed hard. Warm bliss began to spread through my veins. Oh. That was nice. "I'm...not sure I liked it."

He grinned at me. "You're fine. Have another before you decide."

"Okay," I said, holding my shot glass out to him.

"But you have to tell me your story."

As he poured, I shrugged. "I thought you already knew my story. Everyone else does."

"Nope. Contrary to what one might believe, I'm not much of a follower of figure skating."

I giggled at that. "Somehow, I have no problem believing that. Okay, me." I thought for a moment, and as soon as he filled my shot, I held my nose again and drank the next. I gave a little shiver at the burn going down my throat. "Oh, wow. Okay, I think I liked that one more."

"Slow it down, Zara," he said in a husky voice, scooting closer to me. "We've got all night."

Those delicious words burned through me nearly as much as the sake did. I gave him a slow smile, and then my focus went to his mouth. Such a beautiful, full mouth. Hard to believe it had bitten half of some guy's nose off.

"Your story?" he prompted again.

"Right." I put my elbows on the table and propped my chin in my hands. "Well, this might come as a shock to you, but I can be a bit high strung at times."

He clutched his chest, as if shocked. "No! You're kidding me."

I batted my hand at him. "Very funny. It's true. Actually, I was a lot worse during my teenage years because I was also a huge brat. I was super successful really early. I was doing Nationals by the time I was twelve, and

I medaled at my first one. And my next. People thought I was a prodigy, and so did I. I got really, really stuck on myself." I swirled my finger on the rim of my shotglass, and then I licked it. I could get used to the taste of sake, especially if it came with that lovely burn in the stomach afterwards.

"Uh oh," he said, teasing. "I think I smell hubris on its way."

"Oh, it's hubris all right. Anyhow, the 2002 Olympics came up after I'd won Nationals again. I was picked for the Olympic team, and I was the gold medal favorite. I knew it, too. I knew I'd win. I was great at the technical stuff, and I always scored very high on artistry. Judges loved me, and I think it's because I was tiny and graceful. I can fly through the air on a triple like nobody's business."

"I've seen that," he murmured, his voice warm and appreciative.

"I had already planned out my career after my gold medal win. I'd accept a few sponsorships, go on tour, maybe reach out for an acting career, who knows. I was only fourteen, and I had everything at my feet." I sighed. "And then I blew it. I skipped a practice on a crucial day because I saw a penny face-down before I went onto the ice. I don't know if you noticed, but I'm also extremely superstitious."

That sexy smile tugged at his mouth. "The thought crossed my mind once or twice."

"Well, I was an arrogant little shit, remember? So I figured I had my routine perfectly, and if I practiced, I'd just give myself bad luck. So despite Edgar—he was my coach—and his screaming, I skipped it. I knew better than him, of course. I was the great Zara Pritchard." I rolled my eyes at how arrogant I'd been.

"And..." he prompted.

"And of course I fucked it up," I told him. "This story does not have a happy ending. I landed smack dab on my ass in front of the judges' panel. It was the worst. I should have picked myself up and kept going, but instead, I panicked. I was so embarrassed at the thought of me—the amazing Zara Pritchard—bombing out in front of the world that I ran off the ice." I gave him a wry look. "Rule number one of figure skating? Always finish gracefully. Never, ever, ever walk off the ice."

"So what happened?"

I winced. "They booed me. I might have shot the world the bird."

He chuckled.

I grimaced. At least one of us thought it was funny. "I scratched. I was a disgrace to the team. I had to make a public apology for my actions. Penelope Marks won the gold and got my endorsement deals. I got a big fat donut." I made an O with my fingers. "My coaches fired me. So did my manager. I was disinvited from every event I could think of for poor sportsmanship. And I couldn't show my face for years afterward. Still can't, in a lot of circles. I've been blackballed by any figure skater that might have any sort of professional pull, and now I'm too old to start over. So I get jobs where I can. I skate at a mall, give private lessons to kids, and have done the occasional foray as a big, pink dinosaur." I grimaced. "And thinking about all that? Makes me realize I need another drink." I held my glass out to him.

"Damn," he said with a shake of his head. "When you flame out, you flame out good."

"So what about you?"

"What about me?" He grinned and refilled my sake shotglass. "Don't tell me after selecting *Jaws* for our theme music that you really have to ask what I did?"

"Well, no." I watched him fill his own shot, then down it. "I saw a video of what happened. It was pretty brutal."

"Mixed martial arts is a pretty brutal sport overall. That's one of the things I like about it."

"I guess I really just wanted to know why," I began, but trailed off when the waiter arrived to take our orders. My head swimming from the alcohol, I barely glanced at the menu before going with simple—a tuna roll. Ty ordered four kinds of sashimi and a vegetable roll. For some reason, that tickled my funny bone, and I laughed again. "Hungry?"

"Starving, but I'm going to make you try some of it, too." He wiggled his eyebrows at me and leaned in. "Even if I have to feed it to you."

I flushed hot, the mental image of that suggestion sweeping through my mind and doing all kinds of crazy things to my body. Distracting. Which was probably on purpose, now that I thought about it. "Don't change the subject. I spilled my guts. Your turn to do the same."

"I'm not changing the subject," he said, and he leaned back, watching me with a contemplative look on his face. "As far as how that went…well. The guy was an old enemy of mine. Never liked him. Blowhard, rough with his girlfriend out of the ring, just an all-around asshole. He was talking a lot of shit before the fight, and it pissed me off. Like a constant stream of garbage." Ty shook his head. "Then we got in the ring, and he's pulling all these dirty moves. Fish hooking, rabbit kicking me, heel kicking my kidneys, you name it. And they didn't call any of it. Fucking pissed me off. He's making foul after foul and the ref isn't calling any of it." His jaw tightened. "Then he stomped me in the nuts, and I lost my shit. Got furious as hell. Saw nothing but red. So when they called the fight…" He shrugged. "I wasn't done fighting. The ref tried to pull me off of him, so I punched the ref, too, because he was making shitty calls."

"And then you bit the other guy," I said. Seemed like I wasn't the only one with bad impulse control.

He rubbed a hand down his face. "Fucking stupid-ass move. You ever have one of those moments in your life where you can't believe you did something so stupid? And how you pretty much fucked up everything and threw it all away in one hotheaded moment?"

"No," I said sarcastically. "Tell me what that's like."

Ty chuckled. "Right. Forgot who I was talking to. Yeah. It was the stupidest thing ever. I was just so pissed off I couldn't see straight. I think I was more pissed at the ref than at my opponent, but I took it out on the guy I was fighting. Well, mostly. Turned out I bit off a huge chunk of his nose." He grimaced and glanced down at his sake glass. "It was horrifying. I'm still sick that I did it. I paid for his plastic surgery, but it wasn't enough. It'll never be enough."

I knew that feeling. That moment that you realized you were a complete and total fuck up. That you'd gotten so arrogant and so complacent about who you were that let you let it all go to shit because your pride got in the way. And no matter how much you regretted it—an hour later, a week later, a month later—you couldn't take it back.

Ty and I were more alike than I'd thought.

"No," I said softly. "I know exactly what you mean."

He downed his shot and shrugged his shoulders. "I can't take it back, so I'm just working on being a dancing monkey in the hopes that I can repair my image a little. After all, they eventually let Tyson back in the ring, right?"

"Did they?" I didn't know anything about that. "What happens if they don't let you fight again?"

He gave me a blank look. "I honestly don't know. I never had a backup plan."

"Me either. That's how I ended up being a dinosaur on skates."

He grimaced. "Point made. Guess I'll have to think of something, just in case."

I crossed my arms and leaned in on the table, feeling deliciously languid and warm. Alcohol was pretty awesome so far. Why had I avoided it until now? "What do you like to do besides fight?"

He gave me a lazy look. "Fuck?"

"See, there you go. You can start a second career in porn."

"I don't think so. Those girls aren't my type." His eyes glittered as they focused on me.

I sat up straight, suddenly feeling…flushed. And hopeful. "So what *is* your type? I know it's not a stick with a mouth."

"I never said that."

I blinked, a blush creeping up my cheeks. "So what is your type?"

He scooted a bit closer to me in the booth. Marginally closer. Maybe I'd imagined it. But his gaze was on me, flicking from my face to my neck, then back to my face again. "I like them a bit more creative," he murmured, his voice so low I barely caught the words.

"I'm sure there are some creative types in porn," I began, but the words died in my throat when he scooted even closer to me.

"You know what I mean. And driven. I like girls with drive. And I like athletes. I don't even mind if they're high strung."

By now he was sitting so close to me that I could see the details of that little scar in his brow, the sexy dip in the center of his upper lip, and his long, long eyelashes. I was frozen in place, unable to scoot away—and not really wanting to. What was Ty going to do? I'd been closer to him on several of our skate embraces, but this felt like the most intimate thing ever.

He leaned in, and his mouth ever so slightly grazed mine.

I sucked in a breath, and in doing so, breathed him in. He tasted of sake and a unique flavor that I could describe as nothing more than 'Ty.' My lips parted, and he kissed me again, his mouth moving over mine in a kiss that rapidly deepened.

I froze in place, not sure how to respond. Ty Randall was kissing me. Sexy, dangerous, gorgeous Ty Randall was kissing the stick with a mouth. Was it just the sake talking? I didn't know how to react.

"Zara," he murmured against my lips, and his thumb touched my chin, angling my mouth open a bit more. His tongue swept inside my parted mouth.

I moaned against him, caught up in the sensations. God, Ty was an incredible kisser. His tongue slicked against my own, flicking and teasing. My entire body went wild with sensation, my nipples hardening. I leaned into the kiss, curling up against him as he pulled me even closer to him. Under the table, his hand grasped one of my legs and pulled it over his own, his big hand clenching on the inside of my thigh, anchoring me in an intimate embrace.

He made a pleased sound in the back of his throat as I gave in to him, and the kiss grew deeper, Ty's tongue thrusting into my mouth in a way that made me wet between my legs and hot all over.

"Zara," he murmured again, breaking the kiss. "Let's forget about dinner and go home." His hand flexed on my inner thigh, reminding me precisely of where it was.

And I panicked. I pulled away from him, my eyes blinking wide open. "Wait."

He gazed into my eyes, giving me that sleepy-eyed look that was making my stomach do somersaults. "What is it?"

"We can't do this."

He chuckled. "Well, not here, we can't. But nothing's stopping us from going home and picking up where we leave off."

"No," I breathed, and I hated that I had to say it. Hated. I put my hand on his chest. Oh god, he had such a good chest, too. "I mean we can't do this. We can't hook up. Not right now."

Ty blinked at me, as if just now registering my protest. The hand— warm, delicious, big hand—fell away from my inner thigh. "Let me guess. Bad luck?"

It was all that, and more. "We're just doing so well right now as a pair. I don't want to change the dynamic and somehow screw up both of our chances."

Because if we had sex and it was bad? Everything changed. Awkward afterward? Everything changed. Really really great and we wanted to spend the next week in bed? Everything changed. Or if one of us was bad and the other was good? Again, everything changed. No matter how you factored it, sex changed things, and we were in the middle of a competition. We needed to stay the course, not add another aspect to navigate.

He considered me for a long moment, and then gave a heavy sigh. "As much as I hate to say it, you're right."

Part of me was relieved that he wasn't going to fight me on it. Part of me was also…disappointed. He gave in that easily? "I am?"

"Yeah. You and I are both athletes. We know from past experience how sex can fuck up a competitive angle."

Well, *one* of us knew that, at least. "Exactly."

Ty shifted away from me on the bench, and his mouth quirked into a wry smile. "I'm glad one of us has their head on straight, at least. I get it, Zara. We hang in there and keep things going as they are."

"Right," I said, hoping I sounded more convincing to him than to myself. "Staying in the competition and fixing our careers is the most important thing right now."

He poured another sake shot for both of us, and then lifted his up. "To careers and second chances."

I clinked mine to his and hoped I hadn't just made another decision I'd regret for the rest of my life.

Chapter Ten

How am I getting along with Zara? Fuckin' great. She's pretty awesome. If it weren't for this ice skating bullshit, I'd say I could hang out with her all the time and not get bored. —Ty Randall, Practice Interview, Ice Dancing with the Stars

A HORRIBLE BUZZING SOUNDED IN MY EAR LIKE A THOUSAND mosquitos were dive-bombing my brain. It throbbed and ached, and I groaned, pulling a pillow over my head and wishing I could somehow stuff it into my cranium. The buzzing continued.

I fished around in the muddle of my blankets, looking for the source of the infernal buzzing that was making my head ache so badly. My fingers located my phone, set to vibrate, and I squinted at the screen, recoiling at how bright it was.

Naomi.

Ugh. Why was she calling so early? I clicked to answer, raising the phone to my ear, and licked my lips. My tongue felt like a paper towel. "Hello?"

"Wow. Did I just wake you up?" She sounded surprised.

"What's up?" I asked sleepily, wondering why she was talking so loud. Why was everything so damn loud this morning?

"You tell me?" She chuckled, and the noise hurt. I pulled the phone away from my ear an inch, wincing. "I'm on time."

I frowned into my pillow. "On time?" Something wasn't registering.

"You know. Our lunchtime call? Check in with each other, see how our bestie is doing?"

I rubbed a hand on my face. "Lunchtime?" Horror set in, and I bolted upright in my bed, immediately regretting it. My head swam and my stomach lurched. I fought nausea and scanned the alarm clock on the nightstand. It was unplugged. Ugh. Had I done that last night? I held my phone away from my ear and hung up the call just to see the time pop up.

12:06 PM.

Shit!

Scrambling out of bed, I surged toward my closet…and immediately staggered to my knees. Oh god. Oh…that was not good. I was going to barf. My stomach heaved, and I curled into a ball, waiting it out.

The phone began to vibrate again, buzzing. It fell off the edge of the bed, and I crawled over to pick it up. Licking my lips, I answered again. "Hello?"

"Dude, you hung up on me! What the hell?"

Naomi again. "Oh. Sorry." I put a hand to my forehead. "I'm not thinking so clearly right now."

"Are you sick? Do you want me to call a doctor?"

"Not sick," I told her. "Hung over." My first one. *Now* I saw why I didn't drink. I never wanted to again, either. I felt awful. And I'd missed a half a day of practice. Ty was going to kill me.

I peered at my shut door. Where was Ty? Why hadn't he woken me up?

"Hung over? Holy crap, girl. You never drink! Hollywood's definitely changing you." Naomi sounded amused.

"No, it's not. Ty and I went out drinking to celebrate how well we did last night. That's all."

"Oooh, a date?"

I thought back to the kiss—the hot, delicious, incredibly sinful kiss—and gave a long, gusty sigh. "Not really. We're not dating. Can't. Not during competition."

"But you'd date him if you weren't competing? Really? Ty the MMA Biter?" She sounded shocked. "Aren't you afraid he'll like, bite your clit off or something if he goes down on you?"

I crossed my legs and winced. "Ow, and no. He's not like that. He just made a mistake and it fucked him up. You know, like what happened to me."

"You walked off. You didn't bite off half of someone's nose."

"Yeah, but fighting is different," I told her. "The other guy was stomping the shit out of him and pulling fouls, so he got mad. I understand getting mad. And he's totally gentle with me."

"Just be careful is all I'm saying." Naomi sighed. "You're so fragile and all."

Oh barf. "I'm not fragile, you dingaling. You of all people should know that."

"You guys did skate super well the other night," she admitted. "And using *Jaws*? That was a stroke of genius."

"Thank you," I said and smacked my lips. God, I had an awful taste in my mouth. "Listen, Nay, I need to go. I'm late for practice and I'm gross. Can I call you later?"

"Sure, girl," she said, and she sounded incredibly amused. "I'd say 'take it easy,' but we both know you won't."

"Bye, Nay." I hung up the phone and let it drop to the floor, curling up on the carpet for a moment longer. Ugh. I felt so awful. I needed to get up and skate, though. We'd lost half a day already.

Dragging myself to my feet, I swiped at my mouth with the back of my hand. Shower first. Then I'd feel better.

I almost made it to the bathroom before I puked up last night's sushi.

I WANDERED INTO OUR PRIVATE TRAINING RINK ABOUT AN HOUR LATER, still feeling wrung out and wobbly. Ty was there already, skating and practicing his outside edge, arms extended. A cameraman was there, filming him.

As the door shut behind me, he looked up and skated to the edge of the ice, eyeing me. "Damn, girl. You look like hell."

"Thanks," I said dryly, clutching an enormous bottle of water to my chest. "I feel like hell, too." I thumped down heavily on the bench, dropped my water, and began to put on my skates, ignoring that the cameraman had circled back to filming me. "Why didn't you wake me up?"

"I tried to." He grinned at me from the ice. "But you were sleeping so heavily that it seemed a shame to wake you up."

He'd been in my room to check on me? Why had I not noticed this? I jerked on my laces. "We've lost half the day, though. We need every minute for training."

"We'll make it up," he told me easily. "We can just work late if we need to."

I didn't answer. I focused on my skates instead, lacing them tightly and then touching my talismans on the bottom of my skates. I hadn't had time to add something from the skate two nights ago, but I did have a scrap of material tucked into the toe of one shoe, so that would have to do. Satisfied, I removed my blade guards and headed toward the ice and knelt to kiss it.

Ty was watching me as I got back to my feet again and skated onto the ice. I didn't make eye contact, feeling a little weird about last night. He'd asked me to go back to his room, but was that only the sake talking? A post victory high? I felt…weird about the whole situation.

Just imagine how much weirder it'd be if you had slept with him, I told myself, and began to skate the edges of the ice, warming up. Except, that thought didn't make me feel better. Because if I'd slept with him, at least I'd have something to regret. Right now I had nothing but a bunch of heebie jeebie feelings and a lot of uncertainty.

After I'd warmed up, Ty skated toward me. "This week's classical music," he told me. "Classical music and something called a dance lift. You know what that is?"

"Yeah, but those shouldn't be a problem. You already lift me all the time." I tapped my chin, thinking. "The classical part will be the tricky part."

"Cause it's boring?"

"Pretty much. We'll have to think of something awesome this week after last week. We can't go big and then pull back. Audiences hate that."

Ty put a hand to my waist and pulled me close, holding his hand out for me to grasp. "You should know by now that I never pull back."

So many dirty ways to take that. I blushed and gave an awkward laugh. "You know what I mean. We have to make them fall in love with us again. Do you have any particular favorite classical music pieces?" I put my hand in his, and we began to skate, our motions easy after weeks of performing together.

He thought for a minute, and then shook his head. "Only stuff I know is that song they always play at weddings."

"'Pachelbel's Canon in D?'" I loved that song. "Great idea."

"I guess? Whatever it's called. You know, dun dun dundun," he said, and then hummed the wedding march.

I laughed, shaking my head. "That's not Pachelbel."

But an idea was forming in my mind. We were dancing on the ice. Throw on some Pachelbel. Put Ty in a tux and me in a bridal gown with a veil...I gave him an assessing look. "Would you object if we went ultra romancey with this next one?"

He shrugged. "I guess not. I feel like I already checked my man card at the door."

"You're definitely all man," I said, and then wished I hadn't. God, that was embarrassing. Me and my big mouth.

He flashed a grin over at me and dipped me low. "Speaking of me being a man and you a woman....we okay after last night?"

I wanted to straighten my clothes after he righted me, but that would require pulling my hand from his tight grasp, and it'd show just how nervous I was at that question. "You and I are fine," I told him. "We made the right decision."

We did. We totally did. As long as I kept telling myself that, I figured I'd believe it at some point, too.

"I know," he agreed. "Last thing we want is sex fucking up a good competitive pairing."

I said nothing.

"So yeah. Do I think it was the right move? You bet." A pause, and then, "Can't say I don't regret it, though."

"Me either," I told him with a shy smile.

"Well, let's win this thing, then," he told me. "Cause I'd hate to go through weeks of blue balls for nothing."

I laughed.

I NERVOUSLY ADJUSTED MY SHORT BRIDAL VEIL AND CROWN OF FLOWERS, and then looked over at Ty. He stood at my side in his skates, tall and handsome, the long tails of his tuxedo fluttering as he shifted from foot to foot. He tugged at his bowtie nervously.

You'd think the man was getting married for real.

I grinned and put a hand on his shoulder, turning him toward me so I could adjust the bowtie that he'd just twisted off kilter. "Quit fidgeting."

"This is just so…freaking girly." He gave me a sour look. "You realize that every time I get in the cage now, guys are going to give me so much shit for this?"

"Of course it's girly," I told him. "Who do you think's watching this show? And just tell them you got laid a lot after the fact because it made chicks so hot." I smoothed a hand down the seam of his jacket, admiring the way it hung. The man sure did have nice shoulders.

"You think that'll happen?"

"Oh yeah," I teased. "Panties dropping everywhere."

"Yours are staying up," he challenged.

"Only because they're sewn into my dress," I told him, and gave him a flash of the pale pink undergarment that was, indeed, sewn into the lacy froth of my costume.

We'd realized right away that while a tuxedo would work perfectly for Ty, getting me kitted up into an authentic wedding dress would be less easy. For starters, a real veil would just get in the way, so I'd worked with the prop department to come up with a fake lace veil that sat back on a floral crown and fell in a stiff waterfall to my shoulders. It wouldn't move and flutter as we skated, and that was the important part. My dress was a bead-crusted bodice at the top, but the skirt was cut away to the thigh at the front and swept to mid-calf in back. I even had a lacy white garter to complete the image, and I noticed Ty kept staring at it, over and over again.

That made me feel good, despite our vow of chastity.

Of course, now that chastity was on the table, it was difficult to put the cat back in the bag, so to speak. Sexual tension was smoldering between us. It was there in every sultry look he sent my way, every teasing laugh, every joking innuendo. Not that I was innocent, either. I found myself holding onto his hands a little longer when we clasped, or when he'd put his hands on my waist, I'd get turned on. We'd added an overhead lift to the routine, and every time Ty held me in the air, I'd get an erotic charge from the fact that his hands were at the vee of my thighs and from noticing how big and strong he was.

Practice had more or less turned into foreplay.

But we had made it through another week. And as Ty murmured the routines of the other teams into my ear (I still refused to look at the TV monitors and watch for myself), I knew that we had a creative routine. The others had gone more traditional, less exciting. Someone had even worn red, which was a bold choice. Everyone knew that red was an unlucky color.

"You're on in ten seconds," the assistant murmured to us as we stood in the waiting area.

I looked over at Ty. He held his fist out, and I bumped it, then we went through our lucky handshake, getting our mojo on track.

"Go," The assistant said and pointed at the curtain.

We emerged, and the crowd began to cheer. I waved as we skated to the center of the ice, and the roar of the crowd grew steadily stronger. They really liked our costumes. Excellent.

When we got to the center of the ice, I turned and faced forward, tucking my arm in Ty's. He gave my hand a little squeeze and then we bowed our heads, waiting for the music to start.

The beautiful strains of Canon in D began to play, and as it did, we lifted our heads and stepped forward, paused, stepped forward, paused again, and continued to do so in an imitation of going down the aisle at a wedding. When we got to the 'end' of our sequence, Ty took my hands in his and we began to skate. We glided through the routine that I'd mapped out. No flash this time, just pure beauty and sweeping movements to go with the song. Over and over, our hands clasped and we turned in time with the music, our edges tight.

Then came the first partner lift. Ty picked me up, and I felt his grip slip a little. I wobbled, but he recovered, and I kept my body plank straight as we did another turn around the edge, though inside, my nerves were twanging. We'd almost messed up.

But he set me down gracefully, and the audience applauded, and we went on with the routine. The second lift? Went off without a hitch.

We finished the routine in a loving embrace, and the lights went down. The crowd went wild, and I hugged Ty happily. We'd done just fine.

"Sorry about that," he murmured in my ear as we skated forward.

"It's okay," I told him with a pat on the stomach, my head tucked under his arm. "I wasn't perfect either."

"Please. You're always perfect," he told me.

Pleasure rolled through me at his words. Why did such a little, offhand compliment from him make me feel so incredibly good?

Then Chip skated up and gave us both a beaming smile. "Great skate, you two, and interesting choice of themes. I have to ask, though, is there romance blossoming in the air?"

I froze in place, looking up at Ty.

"A gentleman never kisses and tells," he said into the microphone Chip held out for him.

That brought more cheers from the crowd.

"Zara? What about you? Anything you'd like to divulge?" The microphone was thrust under my chin.

I thought for a moment, and then said, "Ty is a perfect gentleman."

A ripple of laughter echoed through the studio, and more clapping.

"Well, with those non-answers, it's now time to see what our judges thought. Let's go first to Penelope Marks." Chip turned to her, and the spotlight shifted from us to the judging table. "What did you think?"

She toyed with her face-down scorecard for a moment. "While I did appreciate the clever twist of the costumes and the pick in music, I found technically that the entire routine was lacking. The lifts weren't clean, and I've seen both of you perform better."

She held up a three.

Boos chorused from the audience, but Penelope's face was impassive. No surprise there. She'd hated us in week one, and she still hated us in week three.

The spotlight switched to Irina, and she smiled broadly. "I thought it was a beautiful theme choice, and I love the costumes. The dance was a little shaky, but we all have bad nights."

Seven.

There was lackluster clapping from the audience, as if they weren't quite sure how to take a seven. It wasn't bad enough to boo, but not good enough to cheer.

"Raul?" Chip asked.

He drummed his fingers on the judging table, thinking. "I agree with Irina. I loved the artistry. However, I also agree with Penelope in that the execution was weak." He sighed heavily, and then slowly turned over his card.

A five.

I clenched Ty's hand tightly, disappointment crashing through me. 15 out of 30. We were going to have the lowest score of the evening. And it was totally unjustified. We had one wobble; that was it. My jaw clenched, I gave another cheerful wave to the audience as we skated away and stepped off back at the curtained staging area.

"Well," Ty said, and looked over at me. "That was bullshit."

"A lot of the time, that's how figure skating scoring goes," I said with a heavy sigh. "They have favorites and make sure those rise to the top, and we're no one's favorites."

"No one but the audience," he agreed. "They fuckin' loved us."

I just hoped it'd be enough.

Sure enough, when we skated back out at the end of the show, Ty and I were in last place. Emma and Louie Earl were in first, Annamarie and Serge were in second, and Victoria Kiss and her partner Toby had slid into third place, a full seven points ahead of us. All of the others had been graded extremely highly. Us? We were like the Bad News Bears of skating.

But we weren't out yet. The audience could still save us. So I smiled and waved ecstatically to everyone and cast Ty a few flirty looks, since I knew they were no doubt wondering if we were a couple or not.

And hey, I wondered that too. So might as well make everyone think about it.

Chapter Eleven

How do I feel right now? No comment. No fucking comment.
—Ty Randall, Ice Dancing with the Stars, Post-Show Interview

THE NEXT DAY WAS FULL OF TENSION. I WENT BACK AND FORTH between being utterly convinced we were voted off and utterly convinced that the audience vote would save us. We'd been charming and fun. How could they not save us? But the judging panel had done their best to sabotage us, and it might not be enough to bail us out.

It was hard to skate and practice when you didn't know if it'd be worth it. But I was an athlete, so I worked my ass off anyhow, and Ty and I worked on practicing some harder elements that we could potentially add to next week's routine.

The hours passed slowly, but then we were off to the studio and dressing in last night's costumes once more. Except now, it didn't feel like as much fun as it had when we'd had hope ahead of us.

As I emerged from the dressing room, Ty saw my face and gave me a hug. "Hey. Either way it's going to be okay, all right?"

I nodded, my throat tight with nervousness. But I let him hug me a minute longer, and then it was time for all of the skaters to go back out onto the ice.

Ty and I were the last couple to arrive, since we'd scored lowest, but I received a perverse sense of satisfaction when the audience cheered louder for us than anyone else. America loved an underdog. Maybe we'd be safe.

"Before I get to tonight's results," Chip said, a fake smile in his voice. "Let's talk with our contestants about how they think they did last night." He immediately skated over to us, and that dreaded microphone was in our faces again. "Ty and Zara. Are you pleased with your performance?"

My mouth worked soundlessly. I knew they were looking for a soundbite, something short that would sum everything up, but my mind was in chaos. I couldn't think of anything clever to say. My nerves were getting the better of me.

Ty leaned in and solved the problem for me. "I don't know about Zara, but I'm not happy with our performance. I messed up, and if we go home, it's because of me. I feel like I let my partner down."

Tears pricked my eyes and I hugged Ty close, burying my face against his tuxedo jacket, oblivious to the cheers of the crowd. "You absolutely did not let me down," I told him. "You were awesome."

Chip moved on down the line and I felt Ty's hand go to my back, stroking it. I didn't pull away from him. I mean, if we were going home, did it matter how I acted right now? So I kept my head pressed to Ty's chest and my arms around his waist because there was no other place I wanted to be at the moment.

A few others murmured answers, but I wasn't paying attention. I was waiting for the moment of truth.

It came a short time later, after a commercial break. "Now it's time for our results," Chip said, and he took the envelope from the tiny skater that came out to give it to him. He opened it slowly, glanced at the audience, and then said, "The first skaters safe this week are…Emma and Louie Earl!"

I straightened, releasing Ty's waist and clapped politely for Emma. She looked thrilled.

"The next team safe is….Victoria Kiss and Toby!"

I clapped again, less happy. We were in the bottom two. No surprise there, but Annamarie and Serge were also in the bottom two, and they'd scored a full ten points higher than us last night. It was clear from Annamarie's unhappy face that she was doing the same math in her head, trying to figure out why she was on the bottom.

Another commercial break passed, an endless moment where we stood on the ice and fidgeted, waiting. Nothing was half as awkward as a commercial break, especially when you were on the filming end with nothing to do.

Then Chip surged into action again. "It's time to announce the team that will be going home tonight."

I clasped Ty's hand, and across from us, I noticed Annamarie and Serge were holding hands, too.

"Annamarie Evans and Serge," Chip began, and then paused for dramatic effect. "You...ARE SAFE. Ty and Zara, I'm sorry, but you have been eliminated."

The audience booed, clearly on our side.

We waved half-heartedly as Annmarie and Serge hugged and skated away, and the closing music began to play. "Do you have anything else to say, Ty and Zara?" Chip asked.

"Thank you for..." I said, and then blanked out again. Tears threatened, and I looked over at my partner helplessly. I was not going to be able to speak around the knot in my throat.

All my hopes had just gone down the drain, along with any chance of a career resurgence.

"We just wanted to say thanks for the opportunity," Ty said, my hand clasped tightly in his. "And that we appreciate all the support we got from the crowd at home." Wild cheers met this announcement, and we waved one more time.

Then it was time to skate off stage.

As soon as we made it back to the curtained staging area, I buried my head in my hands and began to cry.

Ty tucked me in against him, hugging me close. "Shh. It's okay."

But it wasn't okay. I wouldn't be invited back. We hadn't blown anyone away with our routines. I knew that if I had a chance in hell of impressing the producers, I needed to place well. At the bottom of the pack? It wasn't going to cut it. And Ty had lost his opportunity to continue to show the viewing audience how charming he could be.

All because Penelope Marks and the judging panel hated me.

Of course, that only made me cry harder, and that meant Ty hugged me even closer.

"Can we get an interview?" someone asked.

I felt Ty shake his head. "Not right now. Maybe tomorrow."

"We need to do a few wrap-up pieces," someone else said. "For next week's show."

"And I said, not right now," Ty gritted out. "Zara and I don't want to talk to anyone, understand? We'll do interviews tomorrow. For tonight, let us lick our wounds, okay?"

To my surprise, Ty grabbed me behind the knees and hauled me up against him, carrying me. That was fine with me. I burrowed closer to him, hiding my face in his neck, and let him push his way through the crowd of producers, audience members, and cameramen.

Eventually, we made our way out of the studio and to the waiting sedan. "Take us home," Ty said, and the car sped away.

SOMETIME AROUND MIDNIGHT, I PRETTY MUCH GOT ALL THE CRYING out of my system. I was disappointed as hell, sure, but not all that surprised. The moment I'd seen Penelope Marks on the judging panel? I'd known that she wasn't going to cut me any favors. The most disappointing thing was knowing that we'd done well and had creative routines, and that it still hadn't been enough.

But then again, that was the way figure skating went sometimes.

I emerged from my room, tiptoeing into the hallway and looking around. I'd been inconsolable earlier, and despite Ty's suggestions that we go out and party away our sorrows, I'd wanted to come home and just hide under my covers and weep away the pain. So I had. I'd changed into my sleep shirt, crawled into bed, and bawled, alone.

Of course, now that I'd gotten it all out of my system, I wanted to see Ty. I wanted to know what he was thinking, to know how he felt. Had he gone out without me to get over our horrible night? Or had he gone to bed early, too? I didn't think a guy as tough as Ty would be upset over losing like I'd been. Maybe pissy that it hadn't gone well. But not devastated like me.

Maybe I'd take him up on going out, after all. It was only midnight, right? And this was Hollywood. Someplace was bound to be open. I crossed my arms over my sleep t-shirt. It didn't quite cover my panties, and I wasn't wearing anything else, but for some reason, I didn't feel weird about going and looking for Ty while dressed like this.

A weird, thrilling little part of me wanted him to see me in my skimpy clothes. Just to see how he'd react.

After all, this was going to be our last night together. In the morning, the sedan would come to take us both to the airport. No more Ty and Zara. Our team-up would be just a memory, and we'd both go back to our lives.

And if that was going to happen? I wanted to spend tonight with him, even if it just meant sitting and talking on the sofa.

So I headed into the kitchen, looking for telltale beer bottles. Nothing. Disappointment flashed through me. Maybe Ty had gone out without me after all. Maybe he'd already left, since we'd been kicked off the show. Anxiety churned in my gut, and I headed to the living room. "Ty?"

A sound. I turned the corner and saw Ty quickly sitting up on one end of the couch, rubbing his cheek. The leather had imprinted in it, and it was clear he'd been asleep. Across from him, the TV played, but the sound was set to mute, and the local news flashed on the screen.

I stepped forward and gave him a bewildered look. "What are you doing sleeping on the couch?"

He scrubbed a hand down his face again and stared at my polka-dotted panties. Then he shook his head and reached for the remote to click off the TV. "You were so upset. I didn't want to leave you alone, so I thought I'd hang out in the living room in case you woke up."

I crossed the small living room and thumped down on the couch across from him, tucking my legs under me. "Thanks. That's sweet of you."

"It's not sweet," he said. "I'd be a real dick if I just ignored your crying."

"Well, I did shut you out of my room," I said easily, feeling warm at hearing his words. For a big bruiser, Ty sure was thoughtful. "But...thank you."

His gaze slid over my bare legs again. "Yeah." He sounded distracted.

That was a wonderfully heady feeling. I stretched one leg out innocently toward him and wiggled my toes, just to see how he'd react.

Ty got really still. "Zara. Maybe you should put some pants on or something."

I shifted my leg and wiggled my toes against his thigh. Big, strong thigh. Ty was big and strong everywhere, practically bulging with muscles. "Why? What's wrong?"

"Nothing's wrong." He rubbed his mouth and glanced at my bare legs again. "I'm just...human, you know? And if you're not careful, you're going to give me a boner. I'm just warning you."

"Well..." I grazed my toe along his thigh, considering. "Remember our kiss at the restaurant?"

"Oh yeah."

My skin flushed with warmth at the way he said that. Glad to know I wasn't the only one obsessing over that night, and wondering if I'd made the right choice. "The way I see it…we don't have to worry about wrecking our juju anymore. We're out of the competition. So…there's nothing stopping us from kissing again. Or…more. We could always do more." Dammit, virgin mouth, quit talking. "I'm not saying that I just want to kiss. I mean, if you want to just kiss, that's fine with me, of course. But—"

"Zara," Ty said, and he hauled my smaller body into his lap with a swift motion. "Are you coming on to me?"

Embarrassment flooded my body. "Not if you don't want me to—"

His fingers touched my chin. "You know how I said I might get a boner? Already kinda have one. Have one every time you're around. You sitting here in your panties? Fucking killing me."

I scooted closer, my legs pulled over his lap, and I ran a hand along the thick muscles at his neck and shoulder. "You're not just saying that to make me feel better?"

"Make you feel better?" He looked at me like I was crazy. "There are a lot of reasons I'd have a boner, but Pity-Boner is not on the list."

"Just…making sure."

His hand ran down my arm. "For a girl that's so confident on the ice, you sure are skittish in a guy's arms."

Oh god, was I that obvious? How mortifying. "Everyone's got to have a first time at some point."

Ty froze, his hand cupping my elbow. His gaze locked on mine. "What did you just say?"

I swallowed, my throat suddenly dry. "Um, nothing."

He practically recoiled. "Your first time? Zara…you're not really underage are you? Because if I've been creeping on a fourteen-year-old, I'm never going to forgive myself—"

"No!" I smacked him on the shoulder, hard. "I'm twenty fucking five! Do you want to see my driver's license?"

"I almost do," he said, eyeing me. "What kind of twenty-five-year-old hasn't had sex in this day and age?"

I started to crawl off his lap. "You know what? Never mind—"

"Oh no you don't," he told me, grabbing me as I started to get up and dragging me back into his lap again. This time, he sat me fully on his lap, my bottom pressing against him, and I could feel the thick erection in his pants. It made me breathless. One thick arm trapped me around the waist. "Now, explain. Why are you still a virgin, Zara?"

"How many guys do you think I got to hang out with while spending fourteen hours a day on the ice rink? I was homeschooled."

"Yeah, but didn't you crash out at fourteen or something? What after that? You still didn't date?"

"I…kind of had some self-esteem issues after that." There had been years of self-loathing in there. "Pair that in with the fact that the only jobs I remotely qualify for involve ice skating, and there weren't exactly a lot of opportunities to hook up."

"Didn't you ever just go out and let your hair down? Hang out with friends at a club? Meet guys there?"

I said nothing. Naomi was my best and closest friend, and the reason why we got along so well was because we were both socially backward. If I was on the ice fourteen hours a day, Naomi had her nose shoved in a book for an equal amount of time. "Not really good with meeting guys," I said in a terse voice.

"Christ," Ty said, and he lightly tapped his forehead against my back repeatedly, mimicking banging his head against a wall. "A virgin. I so did not need this."

I tried to squirm out of his arms. "You dick. Aren't guys supposed to be excited when a chick's a virgin?"

"Why? I thought we were going to have some sexy, no-strings-attached sex. Now I have to freak out about hurting you because you're a fucking flea, and I'm a big guy."

I rolled my eyes. "You know what? This is really killing my mood right now. Forget I said anything." I tried to get up again.

He pulled me back down once more, and I thumped back onto his lap, earning a small groan from him. "You sure as shit can't go now."

"Why not?"

"Because you're killing me." His hand stroked along the outside of my bare thigh. "Do you have any idea how fucking sexy you are right now? In a t-shirt and these little panties? And to know that you're a virgin? It's a total turn on, and utterly terrifying at the same time."

"How do you think I feel?" I asked quietly. My body was stiff on his lap, but all of my attention was on the hand gliding up and down the outside of my thigh: warm, hard, and utterly captivating. He was callused, the pads of his fingers rough, but I liked that. They were hands that were good at what they did. They matched Ty—a little coarse and uncouth, but tender.

Sexy, no-strings-attached sex? I wanted sex, but I wasn't sure how good I'd be at the 'no-strings-attached' part. He was going to be my first. That mentally had me all goofy already.

His big hand cupped my knee, and then his mouth pressed against my shoulder, through my shirt. "Zara," he murmured.

"You're not going to ask to see my ID again, are you?" I asked, my voice shaky with nerves and desire.

"Nah. I was just giving you a hard time. I watched your Olympics reel on YouTube." He brushed his lips over my shoulder. "When you were fourteen, you looked like you were eight."

I rolled my eyes. "So what were you going to say, then?"

His hand moved from my knee and slid up to the hem of my t-shirt. "I was going to ask you if you'd take this off."

The breath sucked out of my lungs.

Chapter Twelve

She wanted this so badly, and I wanted to get it for her.
—Ty Randall, to his manager

H E WAS LEAVING SEX UP TO ME.
   If I said no, we'd probably cuddle on the couch for a few hours, mope about our loss, and then go our separate ways in the morning. No harm, no foul. I'd remain a virgin, and Ty would forget all about me.

Or I could take a chance and pull my shirt over my head and have a really amazing memory of Ty in bed together with me. We could make love all night long and leave the competition on a mental high note, even if we didn't win.

I knew which one I wanted.

My hands went to my shirt and I hesitated for a moment, and then I sucked in a deep breath. Now or never. I tore my top over my head and tossed it to the ground, and then waited, feeling naked and vulnerable as I straddled Ty Randall's thighs in nothing but a pair of polka dot bikini panties. My shoulders tensed, my back was to him, and I waited for him to do something. Say something. Anything.

One big hand touched my back, and I nearly jumped out of my skin with nervousness. Ty chuckled, the sound low and soothing, and I relaxed at the sound. His fingertips lightly skimmed the rigid line of my back, tracing it. "You're very small," he told me.

I rolled my eyes. How often was he going to bring that up? "I'm not that small."

"You're what, five foot?"

"Five foot three," I told him pertly.

"And a hundred and two pounds. That's small. You're not even a flyweight by MMA standards."

"No?" I was having a hard time concentrating on his words while his fingers brushed along my skin. "What are you?"

"Light heavyweight class," he told me.

I didn't know what that was. Sounded big. Big enough, anyhow. There was no question that Ty was bigger than me—and strong. But he didn't scare me. Every time he touched me—like now—he was incredibly tender and gentle. "Are you trying to frighten me off of having sex with you by comparing our weights?"

He chuckled again. "Not at all. I'm just constantly amazed at how someone as tiny as you can be so strong."

That was flattering. I smiled, glancing over my shoulder at him. I kept feeling the urge to cover my breasts with my hands, but he wasn't looking at them and I was facing ahead, so it wasn't weirding me out so much yet. "I'm an athlete, just like you."

"I know you are. And you're a determined one, too." He leaned in and lightly pressed his mouth to my bare shoulder, sending shivers up and down my body. "I'm sorry I couldn't help you win this thing. I know you wanted it badly."

"It's okay," I told him, and surprisingly it was. I'd gotten it all out of my system at that point.

He pressed a kiss to my shoulder. My skin prickled in awareness, especially when his hands skimmed up and down my bare arms. Was he going to touch my bare front? My small breasts were aching to be touched, my nipples hard and pointing, and I was finding it hard not to squirm on his lap with anticipation.

I needed Ty so much. All the weeks of practice? One long round of foreplay. Now the moment was here, and I wanted him to throw me down on the couch and screw my brains out. But he was going slow, seemingly more interested in soothing me than attacking me. And I liked it...but I wanted more.

I'd simply have to show him.

I considered getting up and turning around, but I wasn't sure if I was that bold yet. So I leaned back and reached out to touch him. My fingers encountered his jaw, rough with oncoming stubble. I tilted my head and tried to kiss him, but it ended up being the side of my mouth grazing his.

That was enough. Ty groaned and kissed me back, the hand locked at my waist tightening.

"Can I touch you, Zara?" he whispered in my ear.

I nodded, more than eager. *Please, please touch me.* My breasts were practically quivering their need.

But he didn't head straight for them. Instead, his hand went to my hair, where it was pinned tight against my head and caught into a rigid bun. I hadn't taken it down when I'd collapsed into tears. "I want to see this around your shoulders," he told me. His fingers tugged at the band holding it tight, and then he frowned. "I'm, uh, just not sure how to get it down."

I laughed and raised my hands in the air to begin undoing the mass of pins holding my hair in place. "It's pretty much anchored to my head at the moment. Give me a second."

"Take all the time you need," he told me. "I'm admiring the view." And he reached under my upraised arm and grazed the curve of one of my breasts.

That sent a jolt rocketing through me. I bit back my moan and concentrated on undoing my hair from the jillions of pins they'd shoved into it to ensure it'd remain in place. I tore at them, anxious to get my hair loose, curious to see what Ty would do—or say—next.

It took me a minute, dragging pin after pin out of my hair, to free everything. As I worked, Ty's hands moved over my back, stroking my skin in a lazy fashion that was utterly distracting, and it made my hands shake just a bit more. Freeing my hair seemed to take forever, but it was finally loose. I scratched at my scalp and shook my curls out to loosen the stiffness from the hairspray, and then let it fall over my shoulders.

"Mmm, much better," Ty said in a husky voice that made shivers move all over my skin. "You never let your hair down, except when you're with me. Did you realize that?"

He made it sound like I was doing it deliberately. Or was that just a double entendre? I didn't know how to answer.

I didn't need to, apparently. Ty's hand grazed over my lower back, close to the band of my panties. "You have the sexiest lower back I think I've ever seen."

That struck me as weirdly specific, and I couldn't help the nervous giggle that erupted. "Lower back? That's…random."

"Not random at all," he said, and I could hear the smile in his voice. His fingertips brushed over my tailbone. "You have the cutest, tightest little butt that flares out. Just above, you have these two dimples at the base of your spine. It's gorgeous. Makes me want to put my mouth there."

I gave a little wiggle in his lap, aroused by that mental image. "What's stopping you?"

"Oh, I plan on it. It's just further down on the list of places I want to put my mouth."

"You have a list?" I asked breathlessly.

"I do. I've been planning this list for days. Maybe even weeks."

Really? He'd been thinking about sleeping with me for that long? "What's first on this list?"

"Your mouth, obviously."

I grinned, my fingers going to my lips. "An obvious choice. I'm disappointed by your lack of imagination."

"Give a guy a minute," Ty said, unruffled by my criticism. "You haven't heard the entire list." And his thumb skimmed along the band of my panties, dipping in to graze at my flesh.

"I'm sorry," I said, in a tone that was anything but. "Please go on."

"Well, once I kiss your mouth to shut you up—"

"Oooh—"

"—I'd go for your ears. You have such soft, sweet little ears that it makes me want to suck on them." And his fingers reached through the tangle of my dark hair and brushed at my earlobe.

It was ticklish, and I squirmed. "Mmm. This is sounding better. Keep going."

"Next, I'd probably kiss your jaw. Again, making sure to keep that mouth of yours quiet." At my snort, he chuckled and his hand went to my shoulder, caressing it. "Then I'd probably go here, maybe move on to your collarbones." His hand swept inward, brushing aside my hair and stroking the skin at the base of my neck.

I bit back the moan building in my throat. His skimming touches felt so very good. "And next?"

"Next, I'd have to start exploring the rest of you," he told me. I felt him shift under my legs, and then his big hands slid forward and cupped my breasts. "Starting with these."

I gasped at the twin sensations that shot through my body. My hands automatically went to cover his—I didn't know if I wanted to remove his hands or guide him.

"You have such beautiful little tits, Zara. Fucking love them." He squeezed my breasts and played with my nipples, stroking a finger over them. "I know you're a tiny girl, but these are the perfect handful. Perky, tight, and I bet they'd taste amazing in my mouth."

A choked little gasp escaped my throat. I'd been trying to be so quiet, but he was overwhelming me with his touch, his words.

"Now that's better," he told me, and he rolled my nipples between his fingers. "I was wondering if you were going to be silent the entire time."

I could feel heat creeping into my face. "I...I just..." My hands clenched against his and then I dropped them, deciding that I did not, in fact, want to stop him at all.

"Wasn't sure?" He leaned in and kissed my shoulder, gave my breasts a squeeze even as he pulled me back against him. Now, my bare back rested against his chest. "Trust me, Zara, I want to hear all your responses. Understand?"

I nodded, shy.

"So when I stroke these pretty breasts," he said, and his thumbs brushed down over the curve of my breast. "I want to know if you like it or not. If you're silent, I can't tell." His mouth was so close to my ear that his breath whispered against my skin, making me feel jittery inside.

"I like it," I said softly. "I like it when you touch me."

"Good," he said, and nuzzled at my ear. "Because I intend on touching you quite a bit. We never even finished my list. You want me to go on?"

And he tweaked my nipples again, eliciting another gasp from me.

"Well?" He asked.

"Yes," I told him, and my voice was breathy with need. "Go on."

He nipped at my earlobe, sending sensation spiraling through my body, and I felt his thumbs roll my nipples again. The sound that came out of my throat was not quite a moan, but it wasn't silence, either. "I'd go on," he told me in that low, husky voice that was driving me wild and making me wet. "I'd play with those pretty breasts for a long time, of course, but that's just the appetizers. I'd want to get on to the main course. So I'd keep going. Tease this flat little belly of yours for a bit." His hand lifted off my breast and slid down the center of my ribcage to the curving flat of my stomach, and then dipped into my bellybutton. "And then maybe I'd go lower."

"Lower?" There was a quiver in my voice, and I wanted to roll my hips against him badly, but I forced myself to remain still.

"Oh, definitely lower, Zara," he murmured against my neck. "That's where all the good stuff is. Hidden in these sweet little panties of yours." His fingers brushed over the mound of my sex, grazing me through the fabric. "How can I make a kissing list and not include the main course?"

My thighs clamped together when he cupped my mound. "Ty…I don't know. What if I don't…taste good?" My face burned at having to admit that out loud. But sex was a big intimacy jump for me. Oral sex? It was kind of blowing my mind at the moment, and it made me nervous.

"Baby, you'll taste amazing." His words were easy, reassuring. "You want me to make your first time good, right?"

I nodded, my torso feeling cupped against his. I loved Ty's body against mine.

"Do you trust me?"

Again, I nodded. He was my partner. I'd let him hold me over his head and fling me around the ice. How could I not trust him?

"Then let me show you how good I can make it for you," he told me. His fingers brushed against the waistband of the front of my panties, hinting at what he wanted to do to me. "Okay?"

"Okay," I breathed, my entire body quivering with nerves. God, I was so freaking skittish right now. He was going to get tired of having to encourage me, I knew it. Ty probably had experienced women in his bed all the time. He hadn't been thrilled I was a virgin. But he was also being so achingly sweet at the moment that I hoped this would go on forever.

Ty sucked on my earlobe, his hand massaging my lower belly, and I moaned. I was definitely slick between my thighs, responding to his touch despite my jangling nerves. My pulse had centered low between my legs, and all of the blood in my body seemed to circulate from there with a heavy *thump thump thump* pulsing right at my clit.

I held my breath when his big hand slipped under the waistband of my panties, and I felt his fingers brush against my sex again, exploring. My body tensed, waiting.

And then he slid two fingers down the wet seam of my sex, parting my lips.

I cried out, arching against him. Oh god. That felt really good. I'd touched myself there before, of course—I was no stranger to masturbation. But having a guy touch me there? Totally different—and a thousand times more powerful.

"Ah, Christ, Zara. You're wet as hell, baby." His fingers stroked up and down my folds, teasing, and then circled the entrance of my sex before gliding upward to circle my clit. "Look at you, just dripping with need. So hot."

I whimpered.

He pulled his fingers out of my panties and held them up, showing me the gleaming wetness coating his hand. "Beautiful." And then he shocked me by putting his fingers in his mouth and sucking them clean. He groaned then. "Knew you'd taste amazing."

"Ty," I breathed, my breath getting raspy and harsh with excitement. I wriggled on his lap, utterly aware of the hard line of his sex pressing up against my backside. I wanted him to touch my pussy again. I wanted him to finger me more. I just...didn't know how to ask for it. So I said, "Ty, please," and clung to him.

"I think it's time we head to my room," he said abruptly. "You shouldn't have your first time on the couch, and if we keep playing, I'm not going to be able to walk."

"Oh." I blushed, mentally picturing him over me on the couch. I kind of liked that image.

His hands gestured for me to get up off of his lap, so I did, feeling a little bereft. My arms crossed over my breasts protectively as I stood, waiting for him to lead the way.

Ty got to his feet, and he immediately turned me and drew me against him. "Don't look so sad, Zara. We're not even close to done."

"I'm not sad—" I protested, but he shut me down with a hot, seeking kiss. I moaned against his mouth, my arms going around his neck. I could taste myself on his lips, and that was wildly erotic, as much as the press of his cock against my belly. My nipples grazed his t-shirt and I whimpered, even as the kiss deepened. He was such a good kisser—when his mouth was on mine, I forgot everything else.

He was also a distracting kisser. Before I knew it, we were at the doorway to his room and I pulled away in a daze, glancing around. Dirty clothes were strewn everywhere, and the blankets at the foot of his bed were crumpled into a pile. Typical guy.

"Sorry," he told me. "Maybe we should have gone to your room."

I thought of my mascara and tear-stained pillow that was totally wet from crying and probably a good bit of slobber, since that went hand-in-hand with sobbing. "Here's fine," I told him.

His hands immediately reached for my breasts again, tugging my nipples between his fingers, and I moaned again, my fingers digging into his shoulders. "Oh. Ty…I…"

"You like that, Zara?" He continued to kiss me, hard, quick little kisses even as he played with my breasts, driving me wild. "Such a sexy, pretty little body. Love seeing you topless like this, with your hair everywhere."

I gave him a dazed look, my fingers stroking his jaw, and then curling around his neck. "You do?"

"Yeah. Makes me think I'll skip the list and go straight for the good stuff." And he gave me a little push, moving me toward the bed. "Lay down."

I fell back onto the bed breathlessly, my breasts bouncing as I thumped, and I noticed the gleam in his eyes as he watched them move. That gave me an entirely different kind of rush, and as I laid back, I stretched my arms over my head, arching my back so my breasts would point at the ceiling, little needy peaks of want.

This time, it was Ty that groaned. "You little minx. I need to taste those right now."

I felt the bed sag as he climbed atop it, and he moved to my side, propping up on an elbow. With one big hand, he pulled me toward him, and he immediately planted his mouth onto the tip of one breast.

I sucked in a breath at the shock that rippled through me. Oh wow. "Ty," I breathed. "Oh god."

"I've got you," he told me, lips moving against my nipple. He brushed his mouth back and forth against it, tickling me, and then gave it a long, slow lick that made my toes curl, and I got wet all over again. "Love these sweet little tits."

My hands clenched and fluttered, and I wasn't sure where to put them. I settled for putting my fists on his shoulders, wanting to somehow touch him but not distract him. I wanted him to keep going.

Luckily, Ty wasn't about to stop. He cupped my breast and lifted it for his mouth to feast on, and I whimpered again when I felt his teeth graze over my nipple. He gave it a tiny nip, and then sucked away the jolt of pain, and then he moved to my other breast, giving it the same attention.

I moaned and clung to him, my hands digging into his shirt and fisting the material. I was going to stretch the hell out of it. I didn't much care, either. This was incredible. I arched my back again, pressing my breasts against him, needing more.

"That's my Zara," he told me, voice muffled as his mouth continued to graze my flesh. His hand released my breast and began to trail down my belly, even as he continued to lean over me and nibble at my nipples, teasing them into stiff, aching peaks.

Then his hand slipped into my panties again, stroking through my slick flesh. He rubbed tiny circles against my clit with his finger, I arched against him again, whimpering as his fingers worked at my pussy, even as his mouth teased my breast.

My hips flexed, and I started to buck against his hand, unable to help myself. My orgasm was getting close, and we were still in the heavy petting stage. "Ty," I moaned. "Ty, please…"

To my dismay, he pulled his hand out of my panties, and I let out a small whimper of protest. He lifted his head and grinned at me, and then leaned in to give me another furious kiss that had me panting for more. "Let's get those panties off of you."

At this point, he could have ripped them off with his teeth and I wouldn't have cared. I needed him desperately, and my orgasm, which had been so close, was ebbing away fast. As he got up off the bed, I reached down and slid my panties off my legs, then shimmied them onto the floor with a kick of one leg. I was totally naked and on Ty Randall's bed.

And he was still fully clothed.

I sat up on my elbows, blinking at him. "Are you going to undress?"

"Absolutely."

"Good," I told him. "I want to explore you, too."

That made him pause, and he grinned even as he pulled his t-shirt over his head. "You want to check me out—all you have to do is say so. I am more than happy to oblige." His hands went to the belt at the waist of his jeans, and he loosed it as I sat there, watching, rapt. Then the belt was unhooked, and he undid his zipper, and his jeans fell to the ground, presenting me with a pair of white boxer briefs that were stretched to the limit over his erection. The front of his shorts were wet in spots where the head of his cock had rubbed against them.

My mouth went dry. He looked…huge. Like, I knew things worked thanks to nature and Cinemax and all, but was it just me, or was Ty bigger than most guys? I had no comparisons to make, but he seemed rather large at the moment, and I was rather…not.

Then his boxer briefs went to the floor.

I stared. I couldn't help it. I'd seen dick in movies and on the internet— who hasn't? But seeing it up close and personal and waiting to go between my legs? Kinda put a different perspective on things. Ty was, well, hung. His cock was big and thick, and there was a large vein running along the underside down to his balls. The head was prominent and nearly dark purple. As I watched, a bead of pre-cum appeared and slid down the crown.

I licked my lips and glanced back up at him. His gaze was intently focused on me, though he wasn't making a move toward me in the slightest.

"Well," I said, tilting my head. "That's…impressive."

Ty chuckled. "I could get used to hearing that."

"I'm surprised you don't hear that a lot," I admitted.

"Oh, I do. I just like hearing it from you."

I frowned, because he'd just admitted that he'd had a lot of partners. God, no wonder he'd been all disappointed when he heard I was a virgin. Was I sucking at this? I chewed on my lower lip, concerned.

"I can tell what you're thinking, Zara," Ty said, and sat on the corner of the bed next to me. "You're not good at hiding your expressions like you think you are."

"Oh?"

"Yeah. You're thinking that I'm hating that you're a virgin, right?"

Damn. The man was psychic. "I just…don't want to be bad at this."

"You're overthinking things. I guarantee you won't be thinking about much when my mouth is on your pussy and you're coming, okay?" He reached over and grabbed my hand, and I sat up on the bed, facing him. "You're fine. You're just nervous, and that's to be expected." He gestured at himself. "Now, you said you wanted to play, too?"

I did. I flexed my fingers and eyed him thoughtfully. I wanted to run my hands all over those muscles and bite them. Was that weird? I supposed

I'd soon find out. I got up on my knees and put my hands on his shoulders again, and then slid to his arms. And I couldn't help it, I squeezed them a little. "You're big everywhere, Ty."

"A man loves to hear flattery," he said, grinning. He remained stock still as I touched him, though. Probably afraid that reaching for me would scare me off. Probably right.

I ran a hand down his arm, admiring it. The muscles in his biceps were incredibly well-defined, and even his forearms seemed strong—a thick vein tracing through his arm. There was a dusting of light hair on his lower arm leading to his hand, and I lightly ran my fingers along his skin. "No tattoos?"

"Nah. My managers wanted to give me a squeaky-clean image. No tatts, no piercings, no wild stuff, nothing." He gave an ironic laugh. "Guess how that worked out for me."

"Not well?" I said teasingly, and spread my fingers as I placed my hands flat against his pectorals. They were two well-defined flat muscles here, and I brushed my thumbs over his nipples, wondering if he was as sensitive there as I was.

His cock twitched in response. I guessed yes, he was.

I smoothed a hand down his belly. Utterly flat, without a bit of fat to him. There were little ridges for his six pack, though it wasn't defined quite like a male model's was. He was just strong and thick all over. Masculine. I decided I liked his chest better than a super-sculpted one.

My hands then went to his big, corded thighs, avoiding his cock...or saving it for last. I squeezed his thigh, and then raked my nails across it. I loved his big thighs. Loved how utterly strong he was. "Do you kickbox?"

"Most MMA fighters do, yeah. It's a good discipline for leg offense."

I nodded, sliding my hand over his thigh again. Then I leaned in and pressed my face to his neck, wrapping one arm around his shoulders, breathing in his scent. I wanted to bury myself against his skin, taste him, everything. I licked his shoulder and loved his groan of response. So I did it again, licking hard and then sucking at his skin, even as my nails raked down his thigh again.

I felt his cock jerk against my belly, felt the low groan in the back of his throat. And then I wanted to touch all of him. My hand slid downward, and I hesitantly touched his cock with my fingertips.

"That's right, baby," he encouraged, and his hand stroked my back.

"Touch me."

I grazed him again, and then grew bolder and wrapped my hand around his length. He was thick, my fingertips barely touching as I circled him. I squeezed, fascinated by the feel of him. His skin was velvety soft, and scorching hot, but underneath, he was rock hard. Fascinating…and delicious. I gave him a hesitant pump with my hand.

He groaned, his mouth seeking mine, and he claimed my mouth with a hard, possessive kiss that I loved. I moaned against his mouth, my fingers sliding over his cock again, tracing the head. Pre-cum was beaded there again, and I dragged my fingers through it, and then spread it around the crown in little circling motions.

Ty pushed against my hand, his hips flexing, and I felt him cup my breast again, rolling the nipple against his thumb over and over again. My moans became pants, and I gripped him tighter, stroking him again even as his mouth plundered mine. This was so incredibly erotic that I felt close to coming from simply touching him and having him play with my breast.

When I pumped a third time, though, his hand went to cover mine. "No, baby," he told me in a soft voice, breaking our deep, intense kiss. "You're going to make me come, and I want to be inside you for that."

I nodded, leaning in for another kiss.

This time, though, he pressed a quick one to my mouth and then shifted on the bed. "Lie on your back. I want to taste you again."

I quivered at the thought. Wanting to taste me could only mean one thing. I moved my legs and fell back onto the mattress, and then I clamped my knees together again as he moved over me.

Ty leaned in to give me a kiss, and then began to trail his mouth down my body. Kisses were pressed on my breasts, my stomach, my belly-button—and then he went further south. His hands gently nudged my knees apart, and I spread for him, hesitant at first. At further nudging, I opened wider, and he dropped off the side of the bed, pulling me toward him, where he knelt on the floor. My hips were on the edge of the bed, and my legs dangled over the side. As I watched, Ty lifted one of my thighs and placed it over his shoulder, then the other.

Then, he gave me a wicked, wicked look before leaning in and burying his face in my pussy.

I sucked in a hard breath, shocked by the feel of him down there. I didn't know how to process it at first. It was too intimate. He moved his head a little, and I felt his tongue stroke along my clit, and a ripple of pleasure moved over me. Oh…that was pretty good.

Ty must have noticed my twitching in silence. He lifted his head and glanced up at me. "How we doing?"

"Not bad."

"Not bad?" He raised an eyebrow, and then chuckled. "I know a challenge when I see one."

And his head descended between my legs again. His tongue stroked over my clit again, this time slow and sensual, and then he licked again. The pressure changed a little, and I squirmed against him. His hand clamped down on my hip, holding me in place, and then he continued to do the same motion, licking a little harder, and then faster.

Oh…that was…yeah. That was actually feeling really damn good. My hips rolled of their own accord, and I couldn't help the moan that escaped my throat. He changed it up a little, sucking on my clit in a way that felt totally different, but equally good, and I squirmed. "Ty…"

"Yeah, baby?" I felt his hand shift and move between my legs, and then his finger pressed at the entrance of my core.

"I need…more. I think." My hands clenched at the blankets, desperate to hold on to something.

"I'm going to give you more, Zara. Don't worry." His husky voice was as erotic as his touch, and I shuddered in response. One thick finger pressed into me, and I whimpered, this time not entirely with pleasure. "Fuck, you're tight," he told me. "Let me know if I hurt you."

Right now I didn't care if he hurt me. I just wanted him to put his mouth on my clit again. So I said, "I'm good."

He pushed in and out with his finger, and I sucked in a breath, because that was a different sort of sensation than his mouth on my clit, but it was still good. It made me want to clamp down around him, lock my legs behind his back and hold him there. Ty pushed again and then his mouth was back on my clit, feasting once more.

I moaned when he pushed deep, and then it felt like he had two fingers inside me, and the stretching, pinching sensation happened again. I opened my mouth to complain, but he sucked on my clit, distracting me. His tongue was working rapidly, and the fingers drove in and out of me, harder and faster. An orgasm was building, just on the edges of my consciousness. I clung to the blankets, my hips raising. "Don't stop," I told him. "Don't stop."

The bastard stopped.

I whimpered a protest, but then he was moving over me, coming to press another kiss on my mouth.

"You doing okay, Zara?"

"No," I whined, clinging to his neck. "You fucking stopped, and I was so close."

He chuckled and pressed another kiss to my mouth. "I'll get you there again, I promise. I'm going to get condoms. Be right back." He detangled from my needy grasp and sprinted to the bathroom.

Ty returned a moment later, smoothing a condom over his cock. I barely had time to glimpse it before his body was pressing onto mine again, and my arms gleefully stroked his back, caressing him. My mouth sought his, and he gave me another open-mouth kiss, our tongues tangling even as he shifted, moving his body between my legs and spreading my thighs wide with his hand. This time I went easily, hopefully, desperate to get relief. I wanted that orgasm.

He shifted again, and then I felt his cock press against my entrance. I tensed in anticipation, waiting for him to move. Instead, his fingers moved to my clit and he began to play with it again.

I was so distracted by that touch that I relaxed, pushing against his fingers. His thumb grazed against my clit again, and I moaned.

And then he sank into me.

I sucked in a breath, my body stiffening. That…had not been a pleasant sensation. Something entirely too big and thick felt crammed inside a too small space, and a sharp needle of pain had flashed through my insides.

"You okay?" Ty kissed me again, and then continued to press light kisses on my face. "Talk to me."

"Feels a little…twinge-y," I lied. Felt like a brick had been shoved up into my girl parts. "I'm fine."

"You're still a shitty liar," he told me, and his fingers continued to flick at my clit. "Give it a minute. It'll go away."

"Mmm," I told him, getting distracted by his fingers. "Just don't stop doing what you're doing down there," I breathed. "I like that." And him being stuffed inside me? Was doing weird things to my senses. My toes were curled, and I was getting weird tingles of sensation that weren't unpleasant. It made me want more.

When I shifted again, Ty pulled back and thrust into me. I winced, because that still felt raw, but it wasn't as bad as before. He regarded me for a long moment, not moving again. "Still okay?" There was strain in his voice, and I knew he was holding back because of me.

So I nodded. "I'm good."

The next time he drove into me, it barely hurt. His fingers kept teasing my clit, though, and I was starting to lift my hips with his thrusts. He surged forward again, burying himself, and then began to move in smaller strokes, pumping in and out, hips flexing. That…oh, that felt really good. My fingers dug into his shoulders and I tried to pull him down closer. I wanted more of that.

"Put your legs around me, Zara."

I did, wrapping them around his waist and locking my ankles behind him. That changed the angle of his thrusts, and when he rocked into me again, I gave a startled little gasp, my eyes going wide at the bolt of pleasure. That orgasm was tickling at the fringes again, and I began to raise my hips with him, needing more. "Ty," I breathed, "Oh…it's getting nice again. I like this."

"Good, baby," he told me. "That's good." And he drove into me faster, his pounding thrusts taking on a harder edge.

Within minutes, I was clinging to him, making inarticulate noises of pleasure as he drove into me. I was still searching for that orgasm, pursuing it with every cant of my hips against his, every slam of his balls against my flesh, every flick of his thumb against my clit. I was so close! Why wasn't I coming? I could feel it just out of reach.

Then, Ty shifted again, and his cock brushed something deep inside me when he stroked down again.

And I went off like a rocket. My legs clenched tight around him, and I felt my pussy spasm around his cock as my entire body reacted to the orgasm. I gurgled his name in the most unsexy way possible, and that gurgle turned into a moan as the pleasure ripped through me.

And then Ty slammed into me, hard, seeking his own release, and I kept quivering, the orgasm kept pounding through my veins, and I whimpered even as he stroked harder and harder. Oh god, this orgasm was never going to end, and I was going to die of bliss.

Ty bit out my name, and then he pushed against me, hard, and held there for a long moment, while I shuddered around him. Then, he collapsed on top of me, his skin moist with sweat. He'd come.

And I had come like crazy.

Wow.

I panted in the bed, trying to catch my breath. That was...holy shit. I had no words. Heck, I'd had no words during the latter half of sex, either. I was pretty sure the sound I made when I came wasn't entirely human.

How embarrassing. Even now, my legs still twitched with aftershocks with Ty's cock still buried deep inside me, his big body propped over mine.

He lifted his head, skin flushed, and gazed at me. "Hey."

"Hey." I was pretty sure I could feel my cheeks turning red. What kind of small talk did one make to a guy that was balls-deep inside you? "So, um, thanks?"

Ty laughed, rolling off to the side and then out of the bed. "You don't have to thank me, Zara."

"Well, I thought it would be better than discussing the weather." I watched as he moved to the garbage can and peeled off the condom. He was still hard, which was fascinating. I thought guys went limp right away? Guess not. He toweled his cock off, and then tossed the towel to the ground and headed back to bed with me.

I scooted over to let him in, and he grabbed the mess of blankets, tossing them over us. Then he got into bed, pulled me against his side, and began to nibble on my ear again.

That made those crazy aftershocks start shooting up my legs again. I squirmed, but didn't try to get away. It felt too good.

"So what now?" I asked him.

"What do you mean, what now?" He brushed a lock of hair away from my ear. "You hungry or something?"

"No, I guess I mean...after the show." I wanted to say *what about you and me*? But I didn't have the guts.

"Well...now that the show's over, we go back to the real world and see if we were able to patch our careers."

Back to the real world. Yeah. Not what I wanted to hear, but I wasn't surprised. He was a fighter in Vegas, and I lived in Ohio. We weren't happening. I knew that. I'd known that all along, of course.

And yet, I was still disappointed to hear it. "Yeah," I said. "It'll be weird to go back to our normal lives."

He shrugged. "Has to happen at some point."

It did. I got quiet.

"So how was it?" He asked me. "Your first time?"

"Not bad," I said again, putting the teasing back into my voice.

He laughed, mock-biting my ear. "You're impossible to please, Zara Pritchard. It's clear that I'm going to have to go for round two."

"Round two?"

"Well, yeah. You didn't think I was just going to roll over and fall asleep, did you?" His mouth grazed my shoulder.

"The thought had occurred to me."

"No, I plan on tonight being a wild event of mind-shattering, brain-melding sex. At least, that will be my contribution to the team. How about you?"

I pretended to think for a moment. "I...can put my ankles behind my ears?"

"Oh shit, really?" Ty looked dazed. "Fuck, I'm hard again already."

I laughed. "Would you like a demonstration?"

"I...think I just might."

Chapter Thirteen

Do I regret anything about the show? That lousy scoring system, maybe. My partner? Absolutely not. Zara was amazing. She was the only reason we made it as far as we did. I don't want to hear anyone say anything bad about her in my presence. Ever. Understand? —Ty Randall, to interviewers, Post-Show

TY HAD BEEN RIGHT ABOUT THE WINDOWS IN HIS ROOM; THEY WERE killer. I squinted at the sunlight pouring onto my face, raising a hand to protect myself from the too-bright light. What time was it?

At my side, Ty burrowed his face further into his blankets, and then he pulled me against him, using me as a human shield against the light.

I wiggled out of his grasp. "Can't stay. Have to pee."

He mumbled something and released me, and I sprinted to his bathroom.

I finished my business in there and headed to his mirror to do a quick check of how I looked. In short: awful. I had stubble-burn on my collarbones, a hickey on my neck, and the back of my hair was a poofed up rat's nest. There were circles under my eyes from the lack of sleep, and they were puffy. I also had the dopiest grin on my face.

The inside of my thighs were sore, as were other, ahem, parts, so I took a quick shower to loosen my muscles. By the time I emerged from the bathroom, Ty had his back to the window and was sound asleep again. I contemplated getting back into bed with him.

And then I sighed heavily.

What was the point in getting back into bed with Ty? Last night had been incredible, but it was now morning. That meant that one of the assistants would arrive soon to pick up our luggage and take us to the airport, and we'd go our separate ways. That was it. End of story.

It was best if I just started packing. Get the whole thing over with quickly, like ripping off a Band-Aid. I slipped out of Ty's room and tiptoed across the hall to mine, stark naked. Changing into my typical tank top and leggings, I tied my wet hair into a bun and began to pick up my room, packing my things. As I did, hot tears began to spill down my face.

I didn't want things to be over. Didn't want this to be the last night with Ty.

Somewhere during this competition, I'd fallen for him hard.

And it hurt to realize that it was one sided. Ty had been tender in bed, but afterward he'd definitely said he wanted no-strings-attached sex. That was fine. I wasn't going to do strings. I'd thank him for making my first sexual experience amazing by not making it messy.

I packed my things, cramming dirty laundry into my suitcase, and then lovingly packing my skates in next to them. I went to the dresser, where I'd pulled off one of the sequins from the bridal gown I'd worn in our last competition. I needed to fix it to my skate to increase my juju.

Then I sighed. I needed to be out of here by the time Ty woke up. I could fix up my skates later. There was no hurry, after all. I wouldn't be skating in a competition again for quite some time…if ever.

I hauled my suitcase up and grabbed my cellphone. Melody had left me a text message. *Whenever you're ready to leave, let me know and I'll have the car there.*

You don't need me for the post-show interview?

My boss says that as long as we have Ty, it's fine.

Ouch. *I'm ready*, I texted back.

Great, she sent a moment later. *Car will be there in five.*

I hauled my suitcase to the front door as quietly as possible, not wanting to wake up Ty. I peeked out the window. No car yet, of course. I glanced back at Ty's room. The door was shut. I…wanted to see him one last time.

So I left my suitcase at the door, tiptoed back to his room, and cracked the door silently, peeking in.

He was so gorgeous. A morning scruff of beard covered his chin, and his long eyelashes were visible, little dark fans against his skin. His full mouth was slightly parted in sleep, and he had the pillow trapped in his arms, hunching carefully away from the sunlight spilling into the windows.

He'd been so tender with me last night, so utterly absorbed in making sure that my first time was amazing. And it had been. I felt ruined for every other guy out there. Who could possibly stand up to Ty Randall? I didn't care if he had a reputation for being a bad boy or punching referees or biting noses. That was in the ring. With me, he'd been charming, patient, understanding, and oh-so-gentle.

I'd fallen hard. Like a stupid idiot, I'd gone and fallen in love with the guy that took my virginity and rocked my world. Damn it.

Tears pricking my eyes, I eased the door shut again, saying goodbye to Ty Randall forever.

Zara. Call me. Muy importanta, girlfriend.

I pulled my phone out of my pocket, looking over at my students tottering around the ice. The adults were pushing wheeled garbage cans back and forth to help them stay steady on the ice. "Let's take a five-minute break, everyone," I said. "Free skate if you want to." I skated off the ice and headed to one of the benches.

Two messages and a text. The text was Naomi's, the other two were a number I didn't recognize. I answered the text. *I'm here, Nay. What's up?*

Did you read the Sports section in Mediaweek today?

Uh, no. Should I have? I texted back, my heart fluttering.

Your boy's back in the game. They put him on probation, but he's got a fight coming up next month, it seems. You excited?

Oh. So the whole TV show thing had worked for Ty. Good for him. I glanced at my students at the mall skating rink. It hadn't worked for me, sadly. I hadn't heard a peep from the producers. *I'm excited for him,* I wrote back. And it was true, I was.

How could I not be excited for the guy I was still madly in love with? It had only been a few days since the competition. The only thing the show had done for me was cut me a paycheck, help me lose my V-card, and give me a lot more first-timer students back at the mall, because everyone thought I was a celebrity *now* that I had been on a stupid TV show instead of being merely an Olympian. Irony, thy name is Zara Pritchard.

You hanging in there? Naomi texted me back.

Boy, she sure knew how to interpret a silence. *I'm fine, I wrote her. It's just going to take me some time to get over him.*

I understand. I won't bring him up again. XOXO.

I wrote Xs and Os back to her and clicked off our chat, checking my voicemail instead.

"Zara?" Melody's voice chimed in my ear. "This is Melody Zimmerman, with *Ice Dancing with the Stars*. Can you call me back?"

The next message was Melody, too. Same deal. I returned the call, curious.

"Melody Zimmerman," she answered brightly.

"Hi, this is Zara. You called me?"

"Oh!" She sounded relieved. "Yes! I'm so glad I got ahold of you."

"You are?" My heart gave an excited flutter. Maybe I'd have a job after all.

"Yes! Listen, ratings have been through the roof this year, and so the producers want to do a little something special with the finale."

Uh oh. That didn't sound good. "Something special like what?"

"They want to have everyone participate in a big skate number for the finale show. Bring back all the eliminated contestants and stuff. Isn't that awesome?"

I glanced at my rink full of students, wobbling on the ice. "Um. So what does that mean for me?"

"We'll fly you back out here to the cottages, and you can stay for the next few weeks on us while you practice your routine."

My heart leapt. Outright *leapt* with joy. A few more weeks? That meant more Ty. More alone-time with Ty. More nights in his bed.

More heartache and pain as I fell more in love with the guy and then we walked away again. "I don't think I can."

There was a long pause. "What do you mean?"

"What does it pay?" Might as well be a little mercenary about things.

She got quiet. "Well...you already got paid by the show, I thought?"

"Yeah, but I just signed up a bunch of new students, and I can't just leave. That's my paycheck. If I cancel classes, I lose all those students for being a flake. I can't survive off of what the show paid me." Thirty grand was nice and all, but it wasn't going to last forever.

"Oh. But you need to practice your routine. You're contractually obligated to appear in the finale show."

I gritted my teeth. "Is Ty Randall going to be there?"

"Yes, he is. He actually hasn't left yet. The producers had him doing some press junkets, so it's perfect that he's still in town." She sounded so bubbly and happy. "Everyone just loves him."

Yeah, that was the problem I had. I loved him, too. Too much. "I can't come back," I told her again. "If you can fax me the routine and send me the music file, I'll learn it on my own."

"But…"

"Yes?" I tried to be patient with her. It wasn't Melody's fault I was an ice diva.

"You have to come back and practice," she said in a small voice.

"I'm an Olympic-level ice skater," I told her in a firm voice. "You think I can't learn your TV show routine? I can learn it in a day. I could learn it blindfolded."

"Well, I know, but—"

"Just fax me the information, and I'll fly out in time for the show. Problem solved."

I could practically hear her frowning into the phone. "But what about your partner?"

"Have him practice with Svetlana. She's pregnant, not dead. She can still skate enough to train with him." And she was keeping her job, and I had been the fill in. They didn't need me. They hadn't even invited me to the press junkets. As soon as our team was off the show, they were done with me. I hadn't forgotten about that.

Why do them a favor if they weren't going to do me one?

"I guess we could get Svettie to train with him," Melody said uncertainly. "I need to run this past my boss. Hang on." I heard her cover up the phone, and a muffled conversation ensued. I even heard a few words about 'she's being difficult,' which made me laugh quietly to myself. They hadn't even seen difficult yet. After a long moment, Melody came back onto the phone. "Okay. I'll email you instructions for the routine and a plane ticket. You have to be out here the night before for dress rehearsal and last-minute costume fittings, okay? Not negotiable."

"Got it. I'll have everything learned by then."

"Okay," Melody said, sounding relieved. "You have my number if you have any questions."

"Will do," I said, and I hung up.

Well, shit. I stared out at the ice, not really paying attention as one of my middle-aged students dropped to the ice, laughing, and his garbage can fell on top of him.

I had to go back to Hollywood because the show wanted to parade us out one last time. It just went to show how completely non-essential I was to them. They'd kept Ty there after he'd been voted off and sent him on a press tour. I was just the hired mannequin, so they'd sent me back to Ohio.

Worst of all, they'd wanted me to spend two more weeks around Ty Randall, so by the time I went home for good, I'd be a complete and total mess, instead of just *mostly* a mess like I was right now. I reached down and touched the bottom of my skate, feeling the sequin from my bridal costume.

I'd worn this the last time I'd been in Ty's arms. Well, sort of. I'd actually been in a t-shirt and panties, but I judged my life by skating costumes, and this one would always make me think of Ty. Me and him. Bride and groom.

Tears pricked my eyes as I tossed my phone back into my bag and headed back out to the ice. I skated over to my fallen student, offering him a hand and swiveling to the side to keep my balance when he accidentally tried to pull me down with him.

The last thing my heart could take was two more weeks around Ty Randall. One night with him had fucked me up good.

The ache in my chest, though? It told me that I wanted those two weeks more than anything. But I knew it wasn't smart.

This was safest. This was the quickest path to recovery. This was the way to forget sexy, irresistible Ty Randall and the fact that he'd wanted nothing but no-strings sex.

"Let's try to go around the ice again, shall we?" I asked my students and straightened the garbage can.

Chapter Fourteen

Where the hell is Zara? She's the only reason I agreed to stay on for this dog and pony show they want to do for the finale.
—Ty Randall, to his manager

Two weeks later

MY STOMACH WAS FLUTTERING WITH NERVOUS DREAD AS THE CAR pulled up to the *Ice Skating with the Stars* studio-slash-ice-rink. The parking lot was empty—the big show wasn't until tonight, and the finale show wasn't until tomorrow. The only ones here would be the skaters and choreographers practicing for the show.

I thanked the driver and hefted my bag over my shoulder. In it were my skates, a change of clothing, and my makeup bag. I hadn't packed more for LA since I wouldn't be staying long. Get in, get out, try not to let my heart get more wounded in the process.

The auditorium was nearly deserted, just as I'd suspected. Five people were on the ice, dressed in their costumes for the finale. It wasn't hard to pick out Ty amongst the others. He wasn't the tallest, but when it came to builds, he was impossible to miss. I'd recognize that brawny pair of shoulders anywhere. A faint smile touched my mouth as I looked at his costume. Black pants, tight black t-shirt. I knew what mine would be—a sleeveless peachy pink dress with a full skirt.

Perhaps the producers could see into my heart and sense how much I was aching. That was the only reason I could see that they'd gone with 'romance' as a routine, picking more movie soundtracks. The skate from the eliminated contestants was a montage of famous films that involved dancing, and Ty and I had been stuck with *Dirty Dancing*. I was dressed as Baby, and from his outfit, he was clearly Johnny. We'd be doing a truncated version of the final routine from the movie to the song "Time of My Life."

It was wildly romantic. It made me ache like mad every time the music keyed up. He *had* given me the time of my life. To make matters worse, in that movie? Baby and Johnny went their separate ways. No happy ending for them. I thought of that every time the music keyed up. They'd parted at the end of summer and went their separate ways.

Just like me and Ty.

My gaze lingered on Ty as he skated a circle, still practicing his outside edge. His moves were as clean and crisp as when I'd left, which meant he'd been practicing with someone. Annemarie skated up to his side, dressed in a spangly flapper costume from the movie *Chicago*, and put a hand on his shoulder, saying something to him. I stiffened, and my back went up when he replied and Annemarie tossed her head back, laughing as if he were the funniest thing on Earth.

Well. I could guess who he'd partnered with. Ignoring the sour pit of my stomach, I headed to the back and the costume-fitting area.

"Good, you're here," said the wardrobe assistant. "Come try on your costume, and let's get you out there so you can practice with the others."

"Sounds good," I said automatically, even though it didn't. I was fighting the very real, very strong urge to run away. So Ty had been paired up with Annemarie? I knew she'd been voted off after us. The finale was Emma and Louie Earl versus young starlet Victoria Kiss and her partner, Toby. The two most likable teams left. It made sense, of course. Still, for a flashing moment, I'd have rather had Annemarie in the finale instead of Victoria Kiss, just so she wouldn't have been hanging on Ty.

Not that I had any reason to be possessive. We'd had nothing but no-strings-attached sex, right?

A half hour later, I was fitted into my costume and all the adjustments had been quickly made by the seamstresses, and I re-approached the ice, where the others were still practicing. I knelt and kissed it as tradition, thinking of the handshake I'd done with Ty in the past. That was over.

Then, I skated in.

The others didn't greet me with enthusiasm. Instead, they cast a few sullen looks my way. That was fine. I wasn't here for them. I was here because I had to be. I skated over to Ty and gave him my most cheerful smile. "Long time no see, stranger."

He gave me a narrow-eyed look. "You're finally here."

That... wasn't a friendly tone. "Yeah. I am. Shall we go over the routine?"

"Why not," he said in a brusque voice, gesturing for me to move into position.

I did so, fighting an uncomfortable mixture of irritation and guilt. Ty was mad at me. I wanted to say something, but the lights went down and the others skated off so we could practice our routine. So I swallowed my words and got ready for the music.

Our routine started out the same as the routine in the movie. In the classic scene, Baby puts her arm on Johnny's neck and he runs his hand down her arm. It's an incredibly tender, touching scene in the movie.

It was *nothing* like doing it in person. Shockwaves skittered through my body as I felt Ty's bigger form press against me, and I put my hand to his neck. His fingers trailed down my arm, and my nipples got hard, my panties getting wet as I thought about the last time we'd been together.

You have such soft, sweet little ears that it makes me want to suck on them.

I guarantee you won't be thinking about much when my mouth is on your pussy and you're coming.

I shivered, full of wild, wanton thoughts, remembering when we'd been together in bed.

Then his hand took mine and the music started, a quick-stepping routine that involved lots of footwork and turns. To my surprise, Ty executed it flawlessly, his movements sharp and on the beat.

We quickly paced through the routine, doing a dual spin in the chorus. The ending was a lift similar to the one in the movie, except I didn't have to get a running start. This had been the part that I knew we'd need the most practice on as a couple, but I'd been stubborn and insisted on staying out in Ohio until dress rehearsals.

When I launched into the air, Ty grabbed me, planting his hand at my waist and lifting me overhead. But as soon as I felt his hands on me, I lost my concentration. My form got loose, and it caused his hold to break. I crashed into him, knocking us both to the ground.

So embarrassing. I landed, sprawled, atop of Ty. Once I caught my breath, I gave him an apologetic look. "Sorry about that. I just got... startled."

He gave me another slit-eyed look. "Whatever. We can take the lift out, if it bugs you."

I blinked at him, wide-eyed, and got to my feet. "We don't have to take it out. I just need to practice it again. I'm sure I can get it."

He gave me a wintry look. "So now you're ready to practice? What about for the last two weeks when I was here busting my ass and you ran home?"

He was *really* mad at me. "I told them to have you practice with Svetlana. She's the real ice skater on the show, remember? I'm just the seat filler."

"Svetlana's not my partner," he hissed at me. "Mine fucking ran away." He started to skate away.

I skated after him, ignoring the others that were staring at us. "Why are you mad at me?"

"Why shouldn't I be mad at you? You ditched our team. At least if I had to be stuck here, I was here with you. I've been alone for the last two weeks."

"Really?" I snapped back at him. "Because Annamarie sure looks like she was getting cozy with you."

"She was my practice partner this last week. You know, that thing we've been contracted to do? That thing you were supposed to do with me but ran away from instead? But I guess I wasn't important enough for a piece of Zara Pritchard's time. I'm just a big, dumb fighter, right? Not important enough to keep in the loop for this piss-ant shit."

Wow. He was really mad. "What the hell, Ty?" I followed him off the ice, snapping on my blade guards. He didn't even bother; he just sat down and started unlacing his skates. "I'm sorry I couldn't be here, but I had important stuff to take care of."

"Important stuff." He looked up and sneered. "Nothing more important than avoiding me, right? Can't be seen with Ty the MMA Biter. Heaven forbid."

My brow wrinkled. "What are you talking about?"

He ripped at his laces, and then stood up, one skate halfway off. "Quit acting like this, Zara. We both know."

"Actually, I don't know," I told him. "So why don't you go ahead and share with me?"

"You snuck out of my bed that night. I didn't hurt you. We didn't fight. So the only thing I can think is that you're embarrassed by the fact that you let a guy like me into your pants."

My jaw dropped.

"Yeah. I've heard it all before. Gee, I like you, Ty, but you're one of those guys. I can't be seen with them. Gee, Ty, not right now. Gee, Ty, can you go stand over there on the red carpet?"

"Are you kidding me? You think I'm dissing you?"

He gave me a fake smile and spread his arms wide. "You tell me. You're the one that ran away and refused to come here even though you knew I was here, all alone and without a partner. I must really embarrass the shit out of you. Why else would you nail and bail?"

"That's not it at all," I choked out, horrified.

"Then maybe you tell me what it is," he said caustically, and he bent to rip at the laces on his other skate.

Nail and bail? I'd tried to make things easier on him. The last thing a guy needed was an emotional virgin falling all over the dude that took her virginity. And Ty had said he didn't want more than a casual relationship. How could I possibly assume anything else? *I left because I was in love with you*, I wanted to say. *And you didn't want that, so I thought I'd spare us both.*

But the words stuck in my throat.

"Got nothing to say?" Ty glanced up at me and yanked at a knot on his skates, and then cursed.

"You want to hear the truth?"

"I think I deserve it, don't you?"

The truth is that I fell for you, Ty Randall. That's right. I fell hard. The stupid, naïve virgin fell for the big, sexy jock. Her partner. Stupid, huh? That's rule number one that you don't break in skating—you don't fall for your partner. It was more than just sex to me, and so that's why I snuck out and I left. All because of your stupid 'no-strings-attached' concept. Me being a virgin just made it ten times worse. So I left, because that's not fair to you and what you want.

But none of that escaped my throat. Instead, big, fat tears began to slide down my face. Horrified, I swiped at them with the back of my hand.

He stood up now, wobbling on his skates. "Don't cry, Zara—"

I shook my head. "The routine's good enough. I have to go."

"Zara—"

"Nope," I said, tears sliding down my face. I pushed away from him. "I don't want to talk. I just want out of here."

And I fled the room.

"Zara, wait," Ty called after me. But he didn't come after me. He couldn't—he was stuck in a pair of half-laced skates. Which was fine with me.

I raced out of the building, my bag retrieved from the costume room, and hailed a cab. If the cab driver thought it was weird that a chick was hailing a cab in a poofy dress and a pair of skates? He didn't say a thing.

This was Hollywood, after all. Weirder shit happened every day.

I COULD HAVE GOTTEN THE TAXI-CAB DRIVER TO TAKE ME BACK TO THE cottage I'd stayed at with Ty. That would have been a free room and dinner... but it also would have meant staying in a private cabin with Ty, and I didn't want to hear him apologize for hurting my feelings.

I knew that was what he wanted to do. It's what any decent human being would do. But an apology didn't matter. Not really.

What would happen if he apologized? Nothing.

What would change if he apologized? Nothing.

What would I do if he apologized to me?

Still nothing. He'd still be Mr. No-Strings-Attached and I'd still be the big, dumb virgin that fell in love with the guy. I hurt just seeing him. It wasn't our argument that made me so upset. That could have easily been talked out. We could have explained everything away and walked out as buddies.

But I didn't want to be buddies with him. And that was the part that was punching a hole in my heart. I was desperately in love with the guy.

So I got a hotel room in LA. It wasn't cheap, and it wasn't a nice room, but it was Ty-free, and that was the only qualification I had at the moment.

MELODY SENT SIX FRANTIC TEXT MESSAGES TO MY PHONE THE NEXT day, seeking reassurance that I'd show up for the finale, and that I'd bring my costume and skates with me. I texted her back, saying I would.

Truth be told, I didn't make the final decision on whether or not I'd show until the last minute. I figured—what would be the worst that could happen if I didn't show up? They'd threaten to ruin my career? Already handled by me, thanks. Take back their thirty-grand paycheck? At this point, I was ready to give it back if I didn't have to skate with Ty and have him embrace me and think for even a second that it was the real thing and he really wanted me in his arms.

If I didn't show up, they'd just cancel our portion of the number and find a way around it. Or Ty would skate alone.

It was the thought of Ty skating alone, looking foolish, that made me climb in a cab and head back to the studio for the final beating on my ego. After all, I loved Ty. I didn't want to fuck up this last thing for him. Didn't want to make him look stupid.

I could suck it up and be a big girl for a few hours. I'd smile for the cameras, do my routine with Ty, and then get on the next flight home and drown my sorrows in celery and organic hummus.

I felt a sense of dread as the taxi pulled into the studio. I had my dress tucked under one arm, the skates in the other, and I headed in to meet my doom. I was immediately trapped by the costume people, who were freaking out that I might have wrinkled my dress overnight or stained it. They swept it out of my hands, and then the makeup artist ran forward. "There you are!"

Just as soon as she did, Ty turned a corner. When he spotted me, he stopped in place. "Zara."

"Can't talk, Ty," I said, letting the makeup artist run me off like a chicken. "Gotta get hair and makeup done!"

I barely heard his muttered curse as the door to the makeup room slammed shut behind us, and I was deposited in my chair.

An hour later, my face was made up to the nines, my lips a perfect red bow, my long black hair had been curled into a bouncy, reasonable facsimile of Baby's hair from the movie, and I was in my costume and skates, waiting to go out onto the ice and trying desperately not to get panicky. My stomach was tied in knots. There was no sign of Ty. Either he was in hair and makeup himself...or he'd had the same thought I had and bailed out.

The show went to a commercial break and a production assistant grabbed me by the elbow. "You're coming onto the ice over at the right-hand entrance," she said. "Follow me."

"We are?" Guess I should have gone to practice. "Okay then."

Bewildered, I did as she asked, and I sucked in a breath when I saw Ty standing there in his black shirt and tight black pants, skates on and ready to go behind the curtain.

The assistant held her hand out. "One minute before the number starts, and then you guys are the third pair up."

I knew that. But I nodded and handed her my blade guards. Then I stepped into place next to Ty.

He held his hand out to me as if nothing was wrong, and I took it automatically. Then, his grip tightened on mine. "Good. Now I have you, and we're going to talk."

I sighed. "Do we have to? We're about to go on."

"I think there was a misunderstanding between us," he said slowly. His gaze searched mine. "Why did you leave without saying goodbye that morning? I thought I did something wrong. That maybe I'd hurt you somehow. Do you know how fucked up that made me? Especially when you wouldn't come back?"

I would not feel guilty. Would not. "Sorry," I muttered. "Let's blame that on the virginity." Man, being a virgin had turned out to be a huge pain in the ass. At least I was done with it.

"I just wanted to say I'm sorry. I wasn't nice to you when you came back. I…just don't understand."

I thought for a minute. "Okay."

That had clearly not been the answer Ty was expecting. As the music swelled and the first couple took the ice to start their routine, he moved closer to me so we could continue talking. "What do you mean, okay?"

"I mean, okay. Thanks for apologizing."

"You going to tell me what made you avoid me?"

"I'm not sure that I will. I mean, it doesn't change anything."

"What do you mean, it doesn't change anything?" He exploded. "What are you talking about?"

Someone shushed us from nearby.

"Look, can't we talk about this later?" I held my fist out. "Let's just do your lucky handshake so we can go out on the ice."

"No, we can't talk about this later. We can talk about it *now*."

"Lucky handshake first," I told him, wiggling my fist. "We can't go out on the ice without it."

He looked down at my fist and then at me. "You do realize I made that shit up, right?"

I gasped. "You what?"

"I made it up. You were freaking out."

"Oh my god!" I felt sick to my stomach. He'd lied about his mojo? "I can't believe you! No wonder we lost!"

"SHHHHHHH," someone in production said.

"It doesn't matter, Zara," Ty told me. "It's not about mojo or juju or luck or anything like that. You have to make your own luck."

"No, you don't," I said worriedly, eyeing the ice. Maybe I'd have time for a quick kneel and kiss before we had to skate out...

Ty grabbed me by the arms. "Fine, you want to make some luck? Here's a lucky kiss." And his mouth planted on mine.

I was so startled that I couldn't say a thing at first. But then his mouth licked at my own and my lips parted to let him into my mouth. I moaned as the kiss became quickly deep and passionate, and I wrapped my arms around his neck.

He broke away from the kiss, though, and gazed down at me. "Now, why won't you talk to me?"

The next song queued up and began to play. "Get ready to go onto the ice in thirty seconds," production told us. "You need to be in place."

"I'm not going until Zara talks to me and tells me why she's avoiding me," Ty said calmly.

"I'm not avoiding," I said anxiously, eyeing the curtain. "We should go out on the ice."

"Not yet," Ty said. "I want to hear what the deal is. You cried yesterday. I made you cry. I want to know what I did."

I gave him a furious look. "Do we really have to go over this right now?"

He put his hands on the sides of my face and kissed me passionately again, silencing my protests. When I was dazed again, he released me. "Tell me what's going on, Zara."

"Tell you?" I murmured, staring at his mouth with fascination. It looked dark in the shadows.

"Go out on the ice," the production assistant hissed again. "Right now!"

"Zara." Ty crossed his arms over his chest.

Oh god, this was making me twitchy. "It's not you, all right? It's me.

I got all goofy over you, and I didn't want it to mess things up. I've been falling for you ever since I met you. It's not your fault I'm a lovesick virgin, okay? You said you wanted no strings attached, so I was giving it to you. I left because leaving without saying goodbye meant no strings attached, at all. That was what was fair."

His jaw dropped a little.

"And as for coming back?" I rushed ahead, my words tripping all over themselves. I gave a nervous laugh. "Come back and spend two more weeks in your arms? Falling in love even more? It'd destroy me, Ty. I felt like if I were around you too much, I'd just fall even harder. So I went home to try to forget you. Give you your space. But I'm doing a shitty job of it."

Before Ty could reply, production came forward.

"Go," the production assistant said and shoved us out the curtain. "Get in place now!" The other song—from *Moulin Rouge*—was winding down, and I grasped Ty's hand as we skated forward onto the dark half of the ice rink. The others were on the far end of the ice, and their routine would end away from ours. The spotlights would cut to us when our music came on.

We moved out into position, Ty standing behind me and me in front of him. I bit my lip as we stood, waiting, facing forward in the darkness.

I felt him lean in, his lips brushing my ear. "Maybe I changed my mind."

"What?" My nipples hardened in response to his body so close to mine, and I prayed that my arousal wasn't visible through my costume.

"I said…maybe I changed my mind. I liked what we had…and I missed it when you were gone. Maybe we could give this another try. And attach a few strings."

My heart thudded in response. Soared.

Ty…wanted me? Wanted *more* with me?

Really?

The music changed. The entire ice went dark. It was time for us.

Oh *shit*, they had the worst timing ever.

The spotlight shone on me and Ty, and to my surprise, a ripple of laughter fluttered through the audience. Odd. The music keyed up, and I lifted my arm, caressing Ty's neck, and he began to drag his fingers down my arm, just like in the movie. It sent ripples of pleasure moving through me. Then his hand grasped mine, and he twirled me outward onto the ice.

And I saw why the audience had laughed. My red lipstick was smeared on Ty's mouth.

Chapter Fifteen

I'm back on track for now. Probation. That's pretty good, though I admit that I almost wouldn't have minded if I'd gotten booted. Maybe I'd check out Ohio, see what it has to offer. Open a sports bar or something. Zara's in Ohio, so it can't be all bad, right? —Ty Randall, to his manager

OUR ROUTINE SEEMED TO LAST FOREVER, BUT WE DID EVERYTHING perfectly, even the lift. The audience cheered wildly when the stage went dark, and then Ty and I skated off. We were done with *Ice Dancing with the Stars.* For good.

As soon as we got to the curtained area, I grabbed the hem of my skirt and began to dab at Ty's mouth. "Oh my god. I'm so sorry. My lipstick was all over you."

He chuckled. "Well, I guess that's one way to keep my man-card. Make out with the chicks backstage."

I laughed at the absurdity of it all, shaking my head at him.

His eyes gleamed at me, and he pulled me close. "Now, you and I need to finish our conversation—"

"Zara Pritchard?"

I turned at the sound of my name, and gasped at the sight of the man standing off to one side backstage. It was my old coach, Edgar Maximoff. He'd grown older—and grayer—since I'd last seen him, but the mustache and the helmet of thick hair were impossible to miss.

"Edgar! Oh my god. What are you doing here?" I pulled away from Ty's arms and went to hug my old coach.

"I'm here to see you," he told me, his accent thick.

I frowned. "How did you know I was here?"

He chuckled. "You are on TV, Zara."

Oh. Duh. "I know. I mean…why?" Why after all these years would he look me up? He'd fired me when I'd walked off the ice during the Olympics.

"I got a tip from an old friend of mine—Penelope Marks."

I made a face at the hated name.

He waved a hand at me. "I know, I know. It is all an act for the show. She is actually a big fan of yours."

I gave him a puzzled look. "She is?"

"Yes. She is the one that called me and sent me DVDs of your performances here. You fired your choreographer?"

"Two of the performances were mine," I admitted.

"They were brilliant." He beamed at me, clearly proud. "I saw an artistic spark in you long ago, but it was buried under all of your, ahem…"

"Brattiness?" I filled in. "You can say it. It won't hurt my feelings."

"Youthful exuberance," he corrected, and smiled. He held a business card out to me. "I want you to call me. I am the production manager of an ice show in Las Vegas at one of the arenas, and I'm looking for a head choreographer with a sense of style and an idea of doing something different. Someone that wants to take risks but knows what they're doing."

I clutched the card against me. "I…okay. I'll call you. Of course I will." Shoot, I'd call him as soon as we left here. A job in Vegas? With one of the big, glitzy shows? Choreographing? It'd be a dream come true. And Penelope Marks had set it up?

I peered around, looking for cameras. Was this sincere or was this some sort of weird TV set-up? But no one was around except Edgar.

This was real.

"Good. Good. You call me." He patted my shoulder. "Now go see your young man. He looks as if he wants to carry you away from me."

I glanced over my shoulder where Ty lurked in the background. Sure enough, he was pacing, and he hadn't even bothered to put the blade guards on his skates, which meant he was going to destroy them. And it was clear he didn't care. I gave Edgar another quick hug and a promise to call, and then raced back over to Ty.

"Did you hear that?" I said excitedly. "A job in Vegas!"

His mouth curved into a smile. "Maybe there's something to this mojo shit after all. I'm in Vegas too, remember?"

I did. My heart thudded loudly in my chest at the reminder, and I gazed up at him. "So what were you saying to me on the ice?"

He glanced around, then spotted a door nearby—the makeup room. Grabbing my hand, he dragged me there and then shut the door and locked it. We were the only ones in there.

Ty returned to my side, and then pulled me into his arms. "I was saying… maybe we give this a go after all. Maybe we try with strings attached."

"Really?" I could scarcely dare to hope.

"Seems like the juju has it all worked out for us," he said, his mouth curving into a smile. "You'll be in Vegas, I'll be in Vegas, you like kissing me, I like kissing you…"

It was definitely lucky that we'd both be in Vegas. But somehow, throwing luck in there made me…sad. "I thought we were supposed to make our own luck."

"We should. I'm just basically saying anything that will convince you to not run away from me again." Ty's hands locked at my waist. "I'm kind of wild about you. You're the only reason I didn't quit after day two. You know that, right?"

"I didn't," I admitted. "Although I did wonder why a big macho guy like you was into ice skating."

"They paired me up with this hot little mouthy chick," he murmured, leaning in until our noses pressed together. Then his rubbed against mine. "How could I resist?"

"Ty…I'm crazy about you," I admitted.

"Not half as crazy as I am about you."

"Good," I breathed. "We can be crazy together."

His big hands hauled me up against him, cupping my ass. "Want to be crazy together in a makeup room?"

"Absolutely." My hands curled into the collar of his shirt, and I pulled his mouth down on my own. His hips pushed between my legs, and I wrapped mine around him, careful of my skate blades.

His lips swept over mine, and our mouths melded in a scorching pairing. My tongue flicked against his even as his hand slid up my skirt, searching out my panties. He cursed when he found them sewn into my dress. "Damn it. These fucking costumes."

"I don't know," I told him in a throaty voice. "I kind of dig yours." My hand gripped his ass and I squeezed.

"You're not giving this dress back," he warned me.

"I'm not?"

"Nope," he said, and grasped the crotch of my panties and ripped at the fabric.

I gasped at the loud, tearing noise the fabric made, but for some reason, that only turned me on more. "Well, you're not giving yours back either," I told him. "I'm going to have you dress up as Johnny Castle for me all the time."

"Who?"

"*Dirty Dancing?*"

"Never saw it." He gave me a roguish look. "But I have to say, I like the theme." His fingers slid under the ripped fabric and caressed my skin. "God, are you always this wet?"

"Only when I'm around you," I whispered.

"Then I'm going to have to keep you around me all the time, aren't I?" His mouth fastened on mine, hot and delicious, even as he began to unbuckle the belt on his pants.

My fingers went to the fastenings, trying to help, but I just got in the way. I settled for rubbing the length of his cock through his pants. "I love you, Ty," I told him desperately.

"Love you too, Zara." He kissed me again, and then he undid his pants. Before he let them slide to the ground, he pulled a small packet out of one trouser pocket—a condom.

I raised an eyebrow at him. "Someone was hoping to get lucky."

"We're making our own luck, remember?" He dropped his trousers to his ankles, and they pooled around his skates.

I remembered. My hands stroked his chest, touching and petting him all over as he pushed down his boxer briefs and rolled the condom on. I couldn't stop touching him. This was like a dream. Ty—my Ty—was about to go deep inside me, and we were going to ride off into the sunset together.

Well, more like ride off into Vegas together, but close enough.

Ty kissed me again, his fingers grazing my hard nipples through the chiffon of my flowing pink gown. His cock slicked over my pussy, and I moaned at the sensation of the head sliding through the lips of my sex. Then, he was pushing inside me.

I sucked in a breath, clinging to Ty. It was still tighter than I'd expected, but a moment later, the burn was gone. I pressed my mouth to his throat, licking and sucking at the skin there as he began to pound slowly, rhythmically into me.

I didn't last long. I didn't need to. Just knowing Ty was in my arms and wanted to be with me aroused me to heck and back. His thumb on my clit as he pounded into me? That certainly didn't hurt matters. Ty came a few moments later, and he collapsed on top of me, pinning me to the counter of the makeup station I currently sat on. I probably had rouge and fake lashes plastered to the backside of my skirt. My skates were locked behind his back, still, and I was pretty sure that Ty's pants were still around his ankles. We probably looked like a mess.

Didn't care. Utter contentment swept over me.

Someone knocked at the door, jolting us out of our reverie. As one, we both looked over at the locked door.

"Shit," Ty said. "I hope they don't want us out on stage again."

I giggled hysterically against his neck because that thought was horrifying and hilarious all at once. And it didn't matter, now that the Ty and Zara team were taking their show on the road.

It turned out they did not want us back on stage, after all. Which was good, considering we looked like a disaster by the time we cleaned up enough to let someone into the room.

The next morning, I woke up, tucked against Ty's side in bed. My phone was vibrating on a nearby nightstand, and I picked it up, squinting at the screen. Naomi had sent me a text with a link in it, and I clicked on it, curious.

MediaWeek magazine had run an article overnight. The headline was: EMMA RAWLEY WINS THE TROPHY, BUT SHE'S NOT THE ONLY ONE WHO NAILS IT. The subtitle was: MMA LADIES' MAN TY RANDALL IS HOT ON THE ICE...IN MORE THAN ONE WAY. And there was a gigantic picture of me leaning back against Ty in our signature *Dirty Dancing* pose. My nipples were sticking out against my dress, and I was clearly aroused. My lipstick was smeared on my mouth… and on my partner's.

I figured Ty's man-card was pretty safe after all. It looked to all the world that he'd gone on the show and nailed his partner. Total stud move. I tossed the phone on the nightstand again and curled back up against Ty's side.

"Mmm." He reached for me, pulling me against him. "Something wrong?"

"Nothing at all," I told him sleepily. "Go back to bed."

"Only if you promise to stay." He tightened his grip around me.

I slid my hands against his warm chest. "I'm not going anywhere. Promise."

Coming soon from Jessica Clare...

Bedroom Games
A Games Novel

Want more sexy contemporary romance? Check out the Billionaire Boys Club, also by Jessica Clare!

The Billionaire Boys Club is a secret society of six men who have vowed success— at any cost. Not all of them are old money, but all of them are incredibly wealthy. They're just not always as successful when it comes to love...

STRANDED WITH A BILLIONAIRE
BILLIONAIRE BOYS' CLUB #1 — AVAILABLE NOW!

When a hurricane blows in, a misplaced passport and a stalled elevator brings controlling, cold billionaire Logan Hawkings together with an unusual woman named Bronte. She's unlike anyone he's ever met—down to earth, incredibly sensual, and even quotes Plato. She also has no clue that he's rich...

BEAUTY AND THE BILLIONAIRE
BILLIONAIRE BOYS' CLUB #2 — AVAILABLE NOW!

Real-estate tycoon Hunter Buchanan has a dark past that's left him scarred and living as a recluse on his family's palatial estate. Hunter is ready to give up on love—until he spots an enigmatic red-haired beauty and comes up with an elaborate scheme to meet her.

THE WRONG BILLIONAIRE'S BED
BILLIONAIRE BOYS' CLUB #3 — AVAILABLE OCTOBER 2013!

Audrey Petty's always been the responsible one. The good twin. Successful, dependable, and trustworthy—that's Audrey. At least, she is until she meets billionaire Reese Durham...

About the Author

Jill Myles is the pen name for USA Today Bestselling Author Jessica Clare. As Jill Myles, she writes a little bit of everything, from sexy, comedic urban fantasy to zombie fairy tales. As Jessica Clare, she writes erotic contemporary romance. She also has a third pen name (because why stop at two?). As Jessica Sims, she writes fun, sexy shifter paranormals.

Too many pen-names to follow? Sign up for Jill's newsletter and you'll receive notices of new releases under all three pen names, along with a coupon for a free read.

You can visit Jill/Jessica's website at www.jillmyles.com.

CPSIA information can be obtained at www.ICGtesting.com
Printed in the USA
LVOW07s0904190715

446785LV00007B/872/P